Wyld Magic

Legends of the Lost Tribes
Book 4

By Kitty Lewis

For information, or to order additional
copies, please contact:

Beacon Publishing Group
P.O. Box 41573 Charleston, S.C. 29423
800.817.8480| beaconpublishinggroup.com

Publisher's catalog available by request.

ISBN-13: 978-1-949472-08-0

ISBN-10: 1-949472-08-0

Published in 2020. New York, NY 10001.

First Edition. Printed in the USA.

For Sharon, the bravest big sister and most stunning diva I ever knew.

Miss you xx

19/2/73 - 26/11/18

Acknowledgements

Firstly, thanks to my dad Ian for reading through my early drafts and making sure I didn't go off on too many tangents. Big sisters Tracey and Sharon, for the likes, shares and support; you two are the best sisters ever! Lauren at The Cover Collection for another fantastic front cover, and everyone at Beacon for being absolutely brilliant. Alex, Naomi, Drew, Lisa, Debbie, Jamie and the rest of you; keep those weird comments coming, I have a few more books to write! Kieran and Mia, my youngest readers, I hope you enjoy this one too. Thanks, are also overdue to Nancy, for setting up and running the Facebook page, and Taj for helping out with the advertising for these books. Millie, of course, for being the inspiration I needed to get writing all those years ago – you are forever loved.

Characters

Enkarini – young mage in training

Soris – apprentice mage, Satorus' son

Caiara – young seer and mage

Kandrina – young explorer, Enkarini's older sister

Remlik – scholar, Kandrina's partner

Remlika – sorceress, Remlik's twin sister

Harndak – blacksmith, Enkarini & Kandrina's father

Jindara – Chief of the People

Braklarn – powerful sorcerer, Jindara's husband

Larinde – daughter of Jindara and Braklarn

Onkadal – Vice-Chief of Akram, Jindara's brother and second in command

Devurak – Chief of Pokole, Jindara's brother

Hinasi – Vice-Chief of Bewein, Jindara's sister

Tironde – former Vice-Chief of Astator, Jindara's youngest sister

Semark – Chief of Wirba, Jindara's youngest brother

Satorus – dark sorcerer, Chief of Entamar

Michael – Prince of Oakshire

Xhih'a Piraj – Li Buqua mage

Maldor – Shadow dragon

Aieden – Fire dragon

Teslyn – Ice dragon

Gistran – High priest of the Creator

Glissia – High priestess of Talri-Pekra

Kolena – acolyte of Talri-Pekra

The Mistress – lost goddess

The Tall One – ancient forest god

Prologue

The story so far:

Kandrina and Remlik had become known amongst the People as adventurous explorers after their journey to discover the true nature of the Colourless, once called Lightning Demons, and their foray into the lands beyond the Serpent Hills to the north where they discovered the war-like Li Buqu, a race of lizard people. Once they returned to the People's lands, they began a study into the Pokole Explorers' Guild, long since disbanded. Many of the journals hinted at some dark mystery surrounding the Great Forest of the West, a place respected and feared by the dwarves, and they decided to head out to visit friends in the dwarf lands to find out more.

After a long search through the dwarven archives, they eventually discovered a lost journal written by the famous explorer C, who was the only one of the Guild to return from the Forest. It told of strange spirits called Diyrae, a dark entity known as the Tall One, and a lost soul trapped in the Forest. Because of the journal's age, and sometimes illegible handwriting, they decided they would travel further, into the Forest itself, to uncover the truth. While exploring, they encountered an ancient lost goddess known as the Mistress, who unveiled secrets about both the Forest and Kandrina's ancestors. The old goddess also had a history with the Tall One and promised to help the two explorers escape the Forest.

The Tall One eventually found them and told his own side of the tale, leaving both Kandrina and Remlik confused about who to trust. They decided to follow the Mistress, working on the theory that she had more reason to want them safe than the Tall One did, but their escape plans were thwarted and they were forced to flee deeper into the Forest, led by a strange creature that was once one of the Diyrae. The rest of the spirits reluctantly agreed to hide the two explorers until they could make it out of the Forest, and they spent several days resting and recovering in a sacred glade.

While the intrepid explorers were

trekking through the Great Forest, the rest of the People were experiencing difficulties of their own. Since the end of the Lizard War, many people had become disillusioned with the tribal union and the previously small separatist movement was rapidly gaining support. Chief Jindara, increasingly desperate to keep the tribes together, tried to convince her siblings to stand with her. Unfortunately, two of her three brothers chose to side with the separatists and declared their towns independent tribes.

Further concerns arose when an insane mage took control of the small village of Entamar, using dark magic and deception to keep the townsfolk compliant. Jindara's brother Onkadal was the only one to openly support her, her two sisters had not yet stated which side they were on, and the People were on the edge of turmoil. The two of them made plans to keep the union going, finally overcoming their sibling rivalries and working together.

Rumours of a dark, sacrificial cult had been running rampant through the poor quarters of every town; beggars and orphans were disappearing, and the Chief's husband was running the investigation into the situation. Unfortunately, he was chasing a false lead and ended up in Entamar, following up on a different cult that had recently been revived. An acolyte of the knowledge temple was also curious about the rumours and had questioned the High Priest of the Creator about his opinion of it all. While enjoying a meal with him at a local tavern, she became sleepy and fainted at the table, vaguely aware before her consciousness faded that she was being carried downstairs.

Kandrina's young sister, Enkarini, had been showing signs of magical talent for some time, but when she began studying magic seriously, her abilities were found to extend much further than those of a normal apprentice. She and her tutor visited the temple of Talri-Pekra, the knowledge and magic goddess, to ask for advice. The high priestess Glissia thought that the girl could be a Higher Mage; the last known one had died over two centuries ago, however, and left all her research to the temple. Enkarini was given a key to the Inner Library at the temple, and together with her teacher managed to persuade her father to let her go and study there. She planned to use the Library's resources to look for a way of finding her sister, who she had dreamt about many times, running lost through the Forest.

Chapter One:
The Inner Library

Bright midday sunlight streamed through the domed, stained glass ceiling, casting a multicoloured light over the entrance hall. Four doors led off the hall at the first level, and two staircases swept around the sides to allow access to the balcony, where there were two more doors. These were closed, but the doors on the ground level were all open, allowing Enkarini glimpses of what was inside. One, the door to her left, seemed to lead to an actual library, a room full of bookshelves and comfortable reading chairs. The next opened onto what looked like an alchemy lab, and a waft of sweet-smelling steam issued from the open door. A large, empty space could be seen through the next door, and from the flashes of light and strange sounds, she guessed it was some sort of spell practice room. The door to the right seemed like a sort of lounging area, with lots of chairs and sofas scattered around, and a collection of games on a shelf. The place seemed far larger than it had looked from the outside, and she wondered if it was enlarged with magic.

Enkarini had arrived in Bewein earlier that morning, to start her studies at the Inner Library. Remlika had dropped her off at the temple of knowledge, said she would come to pick her up around sunset to take her home safely, and gone to search the regular library for any mention of the Forest of the West. She had been growing increasingly concerned about her brother's long absence and total lack of communication, and Enkarini had a feeling she would have gone to search for him months ago had she not been responsible for a student.

She was also worried herself; her big sister Kandrina was out there with Remlik, and she knew they were trapped in the Forest, trying to escape a tall, dark being Enkarini thought of as 'the devil'. She had dreamt about them several times, but it was always the same dream; both of them running through the trees, pursued by the devil, an odd creature leading them. There had been a woman in red in some of the dreams, and at first, she had seemed to be helping them escape, but slowly her role had changed. Enkarini got the impression that the woman wanted something from them, and they were also running from her. She had told Remlika everything she had seen in the hope it would help her with her search. She had also mentioned it to High Priestess Glissia that morning, when she arrived at the Library.

"This sounds incredibly serious," Glissia had said. "I will begin searching for texts relating to the Forest immediately, but I regret to say there is very little known about the Great Forest outside of myths. As for your visions, I wouldn't be able to personally interpret them, but perhaps you could speak with a girl named Caiara. She is one of our most gifted students, and she has a natural talent for Seeing. She can usually gain an accurate perception of both her own and other people's visions, through long practice and her innate aptitude."

Enkarini had smiled at that. She had, by chance, met Caiara a couple of weeks ago at the Spring Festival. The two girls had gotten along quite well, until Caiara's mother had arrived to drag her away. An acolyte had shown her where the Library door was, and she had unlocked it with the key Glissia gave her. It had clicked shut again behind her, and she assumed there was some sort of relocking spell on it so that it wasn't left open by mistake. For a moment, she stood near the door, just looking around at the place. She was about to start looking for Caiara when a boy's voice jolted her out of her thoughts.

"Oh, brilliant. It's the amazing tiny prodigy," he sneered. Enkarini turned to see a tall, thin boy with black hair glaring at her, lip curled in disdain. "Who let you in here?"

She glared back. After his snide remarks and nasty behaviour at the midwinter display last year, she had hoped never to see Soris again, but here he was at the Library. "High Priestess Glissia gave me a key." She turned away and walked towards the lounge-type room, just wanting to get away from the older boy.

Soris walked along next to her. "Seriously? She must have been really impressed by your vanishing trick," he said sarcastically. "What really happened? Daddy made a big donation to the temple?"

Enkarini stopped abruptly. "Do I look like I'm from a rich family? My talents are none of your business, Soris. If you can't be nice, just leave me alone," she told him, pushing past him and into the lounge. There were a few other people sat around on the chairs, some children and some adults. A man with waist-length brown hair sat on the floor, playing a dice game with two blonde girls. Ignoring Soris' presence behind her, she approached them. "Hello, can I join you?" she asked, not really caring about the game but wanting an excuse not to speak to the dark-haired boy.

"Sure," said the man. He produced another set of dice for her, and quickly explained the rules. It was a simple game Enkarini had played before, where a player called a number, everyone rolled, and the closest to that number won the round. "You're new here, aren't you?" he asked after a couple of rolls.

She nodded. "I just got here today. My name's Enkarini," she introduced herself.

"I'm Andar," the man said. She looked at the two girls, who seemed completely focused on the dice they held. "Oh, and these two are Jinna and Janna. Don't take offence that they're not speaking to you, they were born deaf and mute," he explained. "They seem to be connected telepathically, though, and I'm trying to teach them to use that to communicate with others."

He tapped one of them on the shoulder and made some gesture. The blonde twins glanced up at him, and then turned to Enkarini and waved. Enkarini smiled back, and struck by inspiration, she grabbed a quill and scrap of paper from a low table nearby, wrote down 'it's nice to meet you' and showed it to the girls. They smiled even wider, took the paper and wrote back 'pleased to meet you too'.

Andar looked impressed. "You know, you're one of the few people to have thought of that. Most people either ignore the girls or talk to them through me."

Enkarini shrugged and smiled. It had seemed the obvious thing to do; leaving them out of the conversation just didn't occur to her. "Have you been here long?" she asked, writing it down for the girls.

"I've been here most of my life," Andar replied as the twins started writing their answer. "I started developing my abilities as a small boy, and my mother couldn't deal with it. From what I remember, she wasn't very bright, and someone had convinced her I was Demon spawn. She sent me to the temple to be 'corrected', but luckily Lokana, the old high priestess, realised I had a gift for magic and brought me here to learn how to use that gift. I've been here nearly twenty years now, and I try to help the newer students when I can."

One of the twins handed some paper to Enkarini, and she read quickly. 'We were left here last year. Our parents had another baby, and were too busy to look after us properly, so they made us wards of the temple. Glissia has been very kind and let us stay here to learn.' She looked up at them all, saddened by their stories. The matter-of-fact way in which they had told them somehow seemed worse than learning that their parents had essentially abandoned them.

Always one to try and make others feel better, Enkarini decided she would be friends with Andar and the blonde twins. She was vaguely aware that Soris had left, probably got bored and wandered off, and sat playing with the three of them for a while. She figured Caiara would turn up eventually, and sure enough, someone called her name from the doorway. She turned, and saw the petite blonde girl making her way across the room, a big grin on her face and an excited sparkle in her dark blue eyes.

"I've been looking for you," she squealed excitedly. "Hi Andar, JJ," she said to the others, making a quick gesture with her hands that the twins returned. "I need to borrow Enkarini for a while, Glissia told me to show her around. We'll catch up with you later."

Enkarini stood, leaving the others to their dice game, and followed Caiara back into the entrance hall. "JJ?" she queried.

Caiara smiled even wider. "Jinna and Janna. Andar's the only one who can tell them apart, and since they're almost always together, most of us just call them JJ." She led Enkarini straight over to the alchemy lab. "You know what this room's for, of course. I heard Glissia talking to Disari, she said you're advanced enough in your alchemy to have free access to the lab at all times. Disari's the alchemy instructor, by the way. She's a dwarf, isn't that amazing?"

"Sure," Enkarini said, trying to feign enthusiasm. Having spent over a year living in a dwarf village while she learnt basic alchemy, dwarves weren't as fascinating to her as they were to others. She was glad to hear that she would be able to carry on studying alchemy here, though; she had imagined there would be nowhere at the Library to practise her potion mixing and had planned to transport herself back to Wordarla's shop every so often. "Who are the other teachers?" she asked.

Caiara made a thoughtful face. "We don't really have any official teachers here, apart from Disari and Arikele, the priestess in charge of the library. Most of the time we can just study whatever we want, but some of the older or more skilled people act as tutors sometimes. Like Andar, he's the one to go to for mind reading and telepathy," she explained. "He taught me how to do mind contact with others safely. I'm sure he'd teach you too if you wanted."

They had left the alchemy lab while they talked, and now entered the library. It was even larger than it had looked through the door earlier, and several people sat reading in chairs. "This is the study hall; all the books are organised by category, so it should be easy enough to find what you want, but if you're not sure just ask Arikele. That's her over there," she gestured over to a small, dark haired woman in dusty blue priestess robes who was perched precariously on a ladder, looking for something on a high shelf. "If you want to take a book out to study at home, just write your name and the book title over there, then cross it off when you bring the book back." Caiara pointed to a long sheet of parchment pinned to the wall by the door. "You already saw the lounge, that's where we can all hang out and talk when we're not studying or practising. I'll just show you the spell practice room, then we can go and catch up."

"What about the other two rooms? The

ones off the balcony?" Enkarini asked.

Caiara looked back at her. "Oh, one of them is the archive where the Wyld Magic books are kept. It's only opened on certain days, and we're only allowed in while supervised. It's to make sure the books are protected, since they're so old. I don't know about the other one, I think it's some sort of meditation room for the priestesses. They're the only ones who go in and out of there, anyway. Come on, the practice room is my favourite," she said, leading Enkarini across the hall.

Enkarini followed, not really paying much attention to Caiara's praise of the amazing practice room. It just seemed like a big, empty space to her, and she was busy wondering about the other, unknown room off the balcony. It being a meditation room for the priestesses didn't make a lot of sense, surely, they had rooms like that in the temple somewhere. She decided to ask around; someone here must know more.

Jindara waited nervously, hoping that Hinasi would not take too long in finishing whatever she was doing. After writing to both of her sisters two weeks ago, Tironde had been the first one to answer, and her letter had told a rather strange story. Hinasi had delayed her response, and when it had finally arrived, all she had said was 'we need to speak face-to-face, but I cannot leave Bewein at this moment'. Jindara, wanting a speedy resolution to the matter, had taken it upon herself to travel to Bewein and meet with her sister.

Finally, Hinasi's new assistant, a young woman with short red hair and an impressive chest, came to show her into the meeting hall. "The Vice-Chief apologises for the delay, Chief Jindara. There has been some difficult business with two shop owners this morning," she explained briefly. Jindara got the feeling that the girl wanted to go into all the salacious details but had been forbidden to do so. *Trust Hinasi to pick a fellow gossip for her assistant*, she thought as they entered the hall.

The assistant announced her, and once she had taken her seat opposite her sister, Jindara started speaking. She had little patience for formal greetings at the best of times and could not bring herself to sit through the tedious nonsense today. "I regret that I must bypass proper procedure today, but this is an urgent matter. I need to know where you plan to stand in this matter of the tribal union; you must know by now that Semark and Devurak have broken away, and Entamar is under the control of a necromancer who has bewitched the people into following him. This is not the time for dalliance and debate, we must take action, soon." She took a deep breath, preparing for the worst.

Hinasi nodded slowly, her eyes fixed on the tea tray that sat untouched between them. "Jindara, I will stand with you to preserve the union, on one condition. All of us need to sit down together and work out a plan for reform before taking it to the People and letting them choose. There are too many people discontent with the way things are now, and I believe that if no changes are made, we can expect this to flare up again in another ten or fifteen years." She looked up and met her sister's gaze. "I also believe that Wirba and Pokole may be permanently lost as members of the union, though I expect they will make an effort to remain on friendly terms with us. As to Entamar, I cannot say, but I think if they rejoin us we will need to put some system in place to ensure the town is properly governed rather than just overseen."

It was not the response Jindara had hoped for, but better than the response she had expected. She knew perfectly well that things needed to change within the union and had been forming the beginnings of a vague plan herself. "I am glad to hear you say it, Hinasi. Though, why do you suppose Wirba and Pokole are lost entirely?" She was genuinely curious, if anything she would have thought Entamar the least likely to rejoin the union.

There was a pause while Hinasi poured out tea for them both, stirring a generous helping of syrup into her own. She appeared to be thinking, possibly trying to find the right words to say. "Semark has changed, sister. He is no longer the timid boy we used to have to protect from bigger and older children; Father's death transformed him into a different person. Whether this is a good thing or not remains to be seen, but I believe he is beginning to learn how to stand alone, to deal with life in

14

his own way, without constantly seeking approval and instructions from others. He has not left the union out of some fit of pique or some ill-informed act of rebellion; he has reached this conclusion of his own accord, and though we may disagree with him, we must respect his decision."

Jindara did not like it but had little choice but to accept it. "What of Devurak?"

Hinasi gave a half-hearted chuckle. "He's a slippery one, isn't he? I was almost offended when he finally told me about it; usually he keeps me better informed than this." She and Devurak had only been born a year apart and had always been the closest of the siblings. It was unusual to hear one criticising the other, as they usually kept any disagreements to themselves. "I have been sworn to secrecy on a few matters, so I cannot give you a full picture, but I can tell you this. Devurak has been planning this for a long while, almost six years. His aims are honourable, I can vouch for that, but require a certain degree of isolation that only comes with separation. He has been gathering mages and scholars for the past two years, gradually setting his plans in motion. I am sure all will become clear to you in time, but it will mean that Pokole is unable to rejoin us afterwards."

"You can't give me any more details?" Jindara exclaimed. That all seemed incredibly vague, Hinasi hadn't really told her anything other than 'Devurak has been up to something for years and won't tell anyone what it is'.

Hinasi merely smiled at her sister's indignant look. "I can tell you it involves Yoscar. That's all, I'm afraid." She sipped her tea and changed the subject. "So, what do you think should be done about this necromancer?"

Jindara sighed softly. She could tell it would be useless to press for more information about Devurak and his mysterious plans; Hinasi could talk in circles for hours without giving anything away. She reluctantly allowed the change of topic. "I believe he ought to be deposed as soon as possible. How this can be done is another matter. My husband is out there investigating at the moment but has found only dead ends so far. The people are reluctant to speak against Satorus, and many of them are bewitched by some spell that makes them trust him. Even those not under the spell are beginning to fall for the man's charms; apparently, he has quite a way with words," she said.

The two women were silent for a moment, both thinking of possible solutions. "Is there some way the bewitchment could be lifted, or cancelled out?" Hinasi asked. "If the magical factor was removed, we would only need to deal with the man's charisma. You know as well as I that confidence and charm can be lost," she suggested.

Jindara nodded. "Braklarn is looking into a counter charm, but so far all he has found are spells that have to be cast individually. It would take far too long to disenchant everyone separately, and Satorus would probably realise what was happening." She had discussed this with her husband on the calling mirror several times, both of them circling around the same ideas over and over, never finding a workable solution.

"That is a problem," Hinasi mused. "I will have my scholars look into it here;

perhaps there are texts in our libraries that your husband does not have. I shall set them on the task as soon as I can."

They quietly sipped tea for a while, Jindara trying to think of a way to bring up her next topic. Eventually she decided to just read out the letter Tironde had sent her and see what Hinasi thought of it all.

"Tironde sent me a very strange letter last week. Perhaps you can make more sense of it than I," Jindara said. She pulled the scroll from her pocket and began reading it. "Dear sister, I sympathise with your plight, and sincerely hope that you and the others can find a peaceful resolution to this issue. However, I regret to inform you that I cannot say where Astator and its fishing villages might stand with regard to the union. Public opinion seems mixed at the time of writing, and my successor is not one to rush into a decision.

"This brings me to a more personal topic; I am leaving to sail north, in search of the continent Trizes. I will explain my reasons shortly, but I am sure you are more interested in Astator. I have left the city in the hands of General Garren, who has both my recommendation and the backing of the people. He was elected from a choice of three candidates with fifty-eight percent of the public vote. He is both capable and confident and possesses a degree of intelligence far above the average man. I am sure he will contact you in due course.

"My reasons for leaving are personal, and I assure you that nobody is at fault or has forced me to leave. As you know, I was never comfortable as a leader and have been at best an average Vice-Chief for Astator. Lately I have been experiencing 'itchy feet', a desire to wander and discover. I have been in regular contact with Prince Michael of Oakshire, and some months ago he requested that I send some of my town's mages to assist with a study of his lands.

"Several mages from Astator and Tabuah applied to go, and I set my shipbuilders to work on a grand vessel capable of the long journey. As they built the ship, I realised I wanted to go with them, to leave behind this life I had not chosen and seek out my own fate. I have sent word to our siblings, of course; each of you deserves a personal farewell. I wish you all the best and will send you letters when I can." Jindara rolled up the scroll and looked up at Hinasi, unsure what her reaction would be, but certainly not expecting to see a wide smile slowly blooming on her lips.

Hinasi reached across to her own table, piled high with scrolls, and extracted one from the pile. "Tironde sent me something similar. It arrived at around the same time yours did, from what you said. I have a feeling she waited until the ship had already sailed and had one of the mages send these out to us magically, so that we would have no chance to persuade her to change her mind." She shook her head, handing the small scroll to Jindara. "Our little sister has managed to extricate herself from this completely, it seems. She does have a point, though; Astator has not exactly flourished under her governance. Perhaps this Garren fellow will bring the old city back to its former glory."

Jindara scanned the scroll, reading enough to see that it was a farewell letter similar to her own. "You have no problem with her dropping off the face of the planet like this, then?" she asked. It had come as something of a surprise to her, but Hinasi seemed to have taken it in her stride.

"How can I?" Hinasi shrugged. "It is her life, after all; what right do we have to tell her how to live it?"

"I suppose. She could have picked a better time to drop this on us, though," Jindara complained. "We are in the midst of a crisis here, after all."

Hinasi gave her a consoling smile. "I wouldn't worry too much, sister. Had Tironde stayed, she would likely have dithered about for months before making a decision regarding the tribal union. I don't know much about General Garren, but from the little I have heard he is quite decisive. I think we will be hearing from him soon, once the people of Astator have reached a consensus."

Jindara swilled the dregs of her tea around the cup. "I shall have to visit Astator in the near future, I suppose. I would like to know what the feeling on the ground is, which way the people are leaning. This needs to be resolved quickly. Onka is becoming frustrated at the lack of action," she said.

"I would make that journey sooner rather than later, then. Onka's frustration never leads to good results. Besides, the end of spring is approaching. Nobody can concentrate on anything once the preparations for midsummer begin." Hinasi poured more tea, calm and collected as always. "Have you any idea when your husband might return? It must be hard on the little one to have her father vanish," she remarked.

Jindara stirred milk into her tea. "He said in his last letter that he would head back within the month. He seems to think there is little else to discover in Entamar itself, and he is concerned that some might be getting suspicious of his inquiries. He says that he will continue the investigation, and he plans to continue his research in the libraries in Tewen, though I suspect he only wants to return because is missing Larinde."

Hinasi smiled faintly. "Of course. Anyone would pine to be away from such a dear child. How is she?"

"Very well, only the other day she started walking on her own," Jindara said proudly.

"Shall we discuss this over a meal? I don't know about you, but I haven't eaten since sunrise," Hinasi suggested. "Come, let's have the kitchens prepare us some food and you can tell me all about Larinde's first steps."

Jindara stood and followed her sister eagerly. She had been stuck with the increasingly stale food from the saddlebags over the last few days; with her preoccupation and desire for speedy travel, she had not wanted to stop at inns along the way. She would have to plan better for her trip to Astator; a few days on old, dry bread was tolerable, but she could not stomach it for the ten days that journey would take.

~~~~~~~~~~~~~~~~~~~~~~~~~~~~~

Enkarini sat quietly, legs crossed and hands on her knees, trying to concentrate. Caiara had been trying to show her how to control her visions; the older girl was quite experienced in helping others with this, and very adept at her own Seeing. She had been practising for so long, she could summon visions while awake, and sometimes even focus on a specific person or time.

Caiara seemed to think that Seeing the

present was easier than Seeing the future, so for practice she had asked Enkarini to concentrate on her father, back home in Tewen, and try to see what he was doing at the moment. She was attempting to focus on Harndak, picturing him at work in his forge, but her thoughts kept straying to her sister.

"It's no good, I keep thinking about Kandrina," she said, frustrated with herself.

Caiara patted her gently on the shoulder. "Don't worry, it takes time to get the hang of this." She frowned in thought. "How about you try for a vision of your sister? If she's on your mind already, it might be easier," she suggested.

Enkarini nodded. "Okay." She settled back into position, took a deep breath and closed her eyes. A clear picture of her sister's face appeared in her mind; pale golden hair and porcelain skin, her mouth curved in a smile and her ice blue eyes twinkling with mischief. She felt a tear run down her cheek as she thought of her sister. It had been so long since Kandrina left, and even when she had been away, she had always found a way to send letters, or contact them, and she had always come home eventually. This time, Enkarini knew Kandrina was in trouble, and might not come home again. A few moments passed quietly, Enkarini putting all of her effort into visualising her sister.

Suddenly, the image in her mind changed. Rather than Kandrina's smiling face, she saw her sister stretched out on the ground, covered in a thin blanket and gazing up at the sky. Enkarini looked around; she seemed to be in some sort of forest clearing, a small pond in the centre of it, and some clothes were drying on rocks nearby. A splash in the pond drew her attention, and she turned back to see Remlik climbing out of it, soaking wet. Kandrina sat up and smiled at him, tossing him another blanket and telling him to cover his modesty. Remlik grinned, wrapped the blanket around himself, and settled on the ground next to her. Just as Kandrina leant closer to him, the scene faded and Enkarini's eyes flickered open.

"Did you see something?" Caiara asked eagerly.

Enkarini rubbed a hand over her face quickly, unsure whether to feel happy that her sister was safe, excited that she seemed to have had a vision, or sad that Kandrina was still trapped. "I think so. You remember I said my sister was stuck in the Forest? I saw her there with Remlik, her friend, and they were in a sort of glade," she told the other girl. "It didn't last long, though, I only saw a few minutes."

Caiara looked impressed. "That's still pretty good. You must have a very strong connection to your sister," she said, a hint of envy in her tone. "I never had a sister, or a brother. Mum says, 'one little terror is enough'." She smiled, but it didn't quite reach her eyes.

"I'm sure she's just joking," Enkarini murmured. She had seen how harshly Caiara's mum treated her at the Festival and had stood up for the older girl after she was accused of casting black magic.

Caiara shrugged and smiled. "Don't worry about it, Rini. Since I gave up caring what she thinks, Mum doesn't bother me much anymore." She almost sounded convincing.

Enkarini shook her head slightly at the nickname. Caiara seemed to shorten everyone's names, sometimes just to their initials. She didn't mind but hoped it didn't get any shorter; being called 'Nee' would be a little strange. "Come on, let's get to the alchemy lab," she said as she stood. She had agreed to teach Caiara some basic alchemy in exchange for her lessons in Seeing. The older girl had struggled with it at first but was starting to get the hang of the basics. Enkarini hoped to get her mixing her first potion by midsummer.

~~~~~~~~~~~~~~~~~~~~~~~~~

The Library was quiet, most people had left for the night, but Enkarini was still wandering through the shelves looking for a book. Yesterday, Arikele had mentioned a book that talked at length about spirits, ghosts and such, and she wanted to read through it in case it had any information about the spirits sheltering her sister. She couldn't seem to find it though and was heading to check the list by the door to see if someone had taken it out when she heard a strange noise. It was a quiet, soft sort of noise, and it seemed to be coming from a few shelves over.

Curious, she tiptoed round the shelves

and peeked down the row. Someone was curled up in one of the reading chairs, their head tucked into their arms, and it sounded like they were crying. Wondering what was wrong, she approached slowly. "What's wrong?" she asked.

"Go away," was the muffled response.

She could tell from the voice it was a boy, and didn't want to leave him upset like this, so she stayed put. "But why are you crying? Has someone been mean to you?"

The boy sniffed, raised his head, and glared at her. The instant she saw his face she recognized Soris. "Yeah, you're mean for staring at me while I'm crying! Get lost!"

Enkarini was confused. The few times she had run into Soris, he had always seemed so aloof, distancing himself from people and putting them down. He wasn't the sort of boy she pictured crying by himself in a library at night. Making others cry, maybe, but what could have upset him like this? She backed off a little and perched on a nearby table. Whoever he was, she didn't think anyone deserved to be on their own while they were so obviously hurting.

After a while, his sobs died down and he uncurled himself. He rubbed at his face with the end of his sleeve and glared over at her. The effect was slightly ruined by the redness around his eyes, though.

"Do you want to talk about it?" she asked quietly.

He attempted to sneer. "Like you'd understand. Won't your daddy be worried about you? It's getting far too late for precious little girls to be away from home."

She refused to let his comment sting, and simply sat watching him. Under the sarcastic tone, she thought she had heard a strain of jealousy when he said her daddy would be worried about her. "Why don't you try me? I'm pretty good at listening," she said. Even if she didn't understand his problem, she knew that sometimes just ranting about whatever was wrong could make someone feel better.

"Why do you even care? Go get on with your own life," he muttered, curling back into his chair a little. "It's not like it matters to you if I have to sleep here every night because Mum's gone off gallivanting and Dad's too busy to notice I'm not there."

Has everyone here been abandoned or ignored by their parents? she wondered. It seemed like she was the only one with a halfway normal home to go back to at the end of the day. At least she had a father who loved her, even if he did get a bit distracted or worried about other things sometimes. She racked her brain trying to think of something comforting to say, or at least sympathetic. "Do you want me to stay with you? At least then you won't be stuck here on your own."

Soris lifted his head and stared at her. "Are you serious? Why would I want you annoying me all night?"

"Whatever," she shrugged. "Have fun crying alone." She slid off the table and started to walk away. Remlika had taught her to transport herself just last week, so she no longer needed to be escorted to and from the temple. She went home most nights, other than when she stayed over in the temple's student quarters with Caiara or the twins, but she had to be outside the temple for the spell to work. There were wards around all temples, to stop mages transporting straight in.

She had reached the end of the shelf when she heard someone scrabbling behind her. "Wait," Soris called. She stopped and turned to look at him. He had got off the chair and followed her part way down the aisle.

He seemed to be struggling with something, and reluctant to make eye contact. "Why are you being so nice? I've never said anything friendly to you, so why would you care about me being miserable?"

Enkarini wasn't sure, but it sounded like an actual question. "I don't know. I guess I just don't think anyone deserves to be on their own when they're upset." She looked at him closely. "While we're being honest, why have you always been so rude to me?"

He shifted uncomfortably, definitely avoiding her eyes now. "I just am. It's not you specifically, I just don't like letting people get close. It doesn't end well."

"What do you mean?" she asked. She was genuinely curious; she knew some people were shy about getting to know others, but she'd never met anyone who didn't want to make friends with people.

"Look, whenever I start liking someone, they never like me back. They've always got more important stuff to do, or they'd rather spend time with other people, so I just end up running after them like some pathetic lost puppy that doesn't realise, he's been rejected. I'm sick of doing that, so now I just don't bother with people. Pushing everyone away to begin with is easier than getting kicked in the face all the time," he burst out.

Enkarini felt her heart break at those words, and what they implied. On impulse, she stepped closer and hugged the boy.

"What are you doing? Get off," he exclaimed, squirming. "Gods, I just said I don't like people getting close! That's not your cue to run over here and molest me."

She couldn't help a small giggle at the expression on his face. "Sorry. It's just what I do, I see someone's upset and I want to hug them." They stood awkwardly for a few moments. "So, you want some company for the night?"

He shrugged and looked away. "Whatever. I guess it would be more fun than hanging around by myself," he said.

She caught the edge of a small smile flickering across his face though and got the feeling he was secretly rather glad she wanted to stay. "You want to practise duelling for a bit?"

"Sure," she replied. They headed across to the spell practice room, Enkarini running through all the spells she knew to decide what would be useful in a duel. She expected Soris would not go easy on her, even though he was glad of the company.

Chapter Two:
Inside the Archive

The sea breeze caught at Jindara's hair, lifting her spirits somewhat. She'd had far too much time to think on the way out to Astator, and her mind had naturally turned to the most pessimistic scenario it could envisage. Braklarn, who had returned from Entamar only a day before she left Tewen and decided to travel with her, had tried to encourage her along the way. It was a good sign that Garren was keen to meet with her, he insisted, and it showed that he would be willing to listen to her, at least. She wanted to believe that, but far too much bad news had come her way recently.

She was on her way to the town hall to meet the new Vice-Chief, while Braklarn took Larinde to see some of the boats down at the harbour. The weather was fine, so she had chosen to forgo the carriage provided for her official visit and walk through the coastal town. She was glad she had, as the people seemed to be celebrating the beginning of the summer season. There were still a few notices left up from the recent election, the faces of candidates or various promises they had made plastered on walls and windows. She wondered whether it would be worth implementing across the rest of the tribes and made a note to ask Garren how they had gone about it in Astator.

The town hall came into view as she rounded a corner, a long, low building that was more of a general meeting place than anything official. She reminded herself that things had always been done differently in Astator; the Chiefs in the past had not been inclined to grandeur or open displays of wealth, preferring to put the people's taxes back into the town. After the merging, with Astator being slightly disconnected from the rest of the People, the Vice-Chiefs had continued that tradition. *Perhaps we could all learn something from Astator's methods,* Jindara thought wryly as she entered the hall. There was one large hall, currently empty aside from an old woman sweeping the floor, and a dozen smaller meeting rooms in the building. Garren had asked her to meet him in room four, so she proceeded until she came to a room with the number four etched into the door.

"Chief Jindara," a man said as she entered the room. She looked at him; tall and thickset, with messy, sandy blonde hair and pale grey eyes. A scar marked his right cheek and his left hand was missing, a carved wooden one fixed in its place. He looked like someone who had been through a lot of trouble and could handle problems with a cool head and steady hand. Just the sort of person she needed on her side right now, maybe he could counter Onka's temper a little. "Welcome to Astator. I hope you had a pleasant journey? The road between us and Tewen can get rather muddy in the spring."

Jindara smiled politely and shook the man's hand. This had at least got off to a good start. "The road was fine, thank you; there hasn't been much rain yet this season. It's a pleasure to meet you, Vice-Chief – or do you prefer General?" She knew some military men preferred to be known by their rank, regardless of any other title they gained after service.

"Either is fine, though many simply

call me Garren," he said, returning her smile. There was a genuine warmth behind it, and she could see how he had won over the majority of the town. "Would you care for some refreshments, Chief? Some tea, or perhaps a light snack?"

"Just water, please; I ate lunch with my husband not long before coming here," she replied. They sat down either side of the small table, and a boy brought in a pitcher of iced water and two glasses. The room was light and airy, if a little smaller than Jindara had expected, and decorated with strings of pebbles and seashells. The sound of the waves nearby lent a relaxing atmosphere to the place. "You must know why I have come to speak with you; I need to know where everyone stands so that we can form a plan to save the tribal union."

Garren nodded. "I guessed as much. Fair warning, I cannot yet say for certain what the people of Astator want, as the debate is still going on. The separatist movement does seem to have lost momentum around here, though. More people are calling for change than for secession now. The union has its problems, of course, I don't believe anyone could deny that," he said. "However, deliberately causing divisions and rifts does not solve anything. I personally am a firm supporter of the tribes remaining together, and I feel that many of my people are, too. I will ask for confirmation of the public's opinion before publicly declaring anything, but it is likely Astator will stay in the union."

Jindara sighed in relief. Garren was obviously a strong leader and would be a valuable ally in the coming months. It felt good to finally speak with someone who was open to listening and could see the sense of what she said.

"I ought to add a caveat here," he continued, raising an eyebrow at her. "I can't speak for other towns, obviously, but certainly in Astator there is a feeling of having control of our own affairs wrested from us. The people do not want this, however friendly they feel towards the rest of the tribes. You, Vice-Chiefs Hinasi and Onkadal, and I need to come together and devise a plan for reform. We need to focus on cooperation, not control. Quite aside from anything else, the tribes are so far apart geographically that there are vastly different issues in each town. For example, concerns about sea floods would barely even cross the mind of someone living in Bewein, yet they are a yearly concern for those in Astator. We here have no issue with the nayrim during autumn, yet those in Akram have to protect their farms every harvest."

"So, each town ought to be free to make its own laws, have the final say over things that affect its people?" Jindara suggested. "I have been thinking along those lines recently. I admit, I cannot imagine spending every winter under the threat of potential flooding, so could not hope to think of an adequate plan to deal with such." She thought for a moment, back to a history lesson she had paid little attention to at the time. "Before Morendir united the tribes, there was some kind of trade alliance between Manak, Tewen, Akram and Bewein. I don't remember all of it, but from what I can recall, it involved open markets, an agreement to band the armies together against outside threats, but each tribe still governed itself. I can look up the details in a library, and perhaps we could use it as a basis for our reforms?"

Garren tapped the side of his glass absently. "I seem to recall something along those lines being mentioned in a history lecture I slept through many years ago. It could at least give us a starting point," he agreed. "I must confess, I am not much of a scholar, but my son always has his nose buried in some book or other. He will know where to look; I can ask him to visit the library with me and find the relevant information."

Jindara smiled and nodded. "I shall ask the same of my husband. He would live in the library given half a chance," she said in jest.

He chuckled. "I know what you mean. I'm sure my boy wishes he had been born a girl, just so that he could join Talri-Pekra's order." He poured out more water, and a sudden frown crossed his features. "Speaking of temples, have you heard any news from Entamar or Wirba lately?"

"Not for several weeks; in fact, nothing directly from Entamar in months," she told him. "Why? Have you heard anything?"

He grimaced. "Heard? No. Seen, most

definitely." He pulled a map of Astator and the surrounding area from under the table and spread it between them. "I've no idea what that mad death mage is up to, but he's had his army marching about on our borders. They spent almost three weeks camped out here, looking like they were preparing to stage an attack." He pointed to a large X near the southernmost fishing village on the coast. "We were so convinced they were about to invade that I had the village evacuated. By the time I got down there with a squad, Entamar's lot had upped sticks and left."

Jindara frowned. "That's bizarre, and certainly disturbing, but why did you mention the temples?"

"They had left a little present behind. There weren't only soldiers there, several of the villagers reported seeing priestesses in black gowns performing rituals in the camp. When we got down there, we found a sacrifice nailed to a tree." He met her eyes, and Jindara realised he didn't mean an animal sacrifice. "The victim had this symbol carved in her forehead," he added, showing her a parchment with a familiar spiral sketched onto it.

"The spiral gods," she breathed. "Braklarn has been chasing this for months, but he kept hitting dead ends. He thought it had something to do with a killer who was on the loose around Tewen and Bewein," she said.

Garren looked interested. "I'd like to speak with him, then. My town watch has been looking into it since we found the poor girl, and they've come across something very odd regarding a schism in one of the old temples, and some involvement with an abandoned dwarven god, of all things. Would your husband be willing to work with them? At the very least, they could share information," he suggested.

"I don't see why not. I'll tell him to contact your watch about it as soon as he can." Jindara drained her glass and prepared to leave. "Thank you for meeting with me, Garren. I look forward to working with you," she said, offering her hand.

Garren shook it, smiling. "It was my pleasure, Chief. I believe we can sort out this mess together and give our children a better future."

Jindara smiled back. That had been the phrase on many of Garren's posters, 'a better future for our children'. She had to admit, it had a hopeful ring to it. She left the hall, feeling a lot better than she had when she arrived.

~~~~~~~~~~~~~~~~~~~~~~~~~~~

Caiara looked around the room, clearly fascinated. "Your father really lets you keep this stuff in your room?" she asked, gazing at the alchemy equipment in one corner.

"Only because we don't really have anywhere else to keep it," Enkarini told her. "The only other place it wouldn't be in the way is the garden, and Father doesn't want to leave it out there since it was so expensive." She shook out the blankets and laid them over the floor. Caiara had finally persuaded her mother to let her stay the night at Enkarini's, and she was barely able to contain herself.

"I didn't realise alchemy equipment was expensive," Caiara said. "It's basically just a cauldron, and leaves and stuff, isn't it?"

Enkarini shook her head. She'd been

43

trying to teach Caiara basic alchemy for three weeks now, and the older girl hadn't even grasped the simplest things. She knew she'd learned quicker than most people did, but she thought that after three weeks anyone could at least be able to do the click flame. "There are lots of different cauldrons, because some potions can only be mixed properly in certain conditions. I explained all that last week," she teased gently. "Then there are the ingredients, some are just leaves from the garden but others are really hard to get or have to be prepared in a particular way. Add in the stirrers, vials to keep the mixed potions in, stuff for cutting and grinding and everything, it all costs a fortune." She paused, realising how much like her father she had sounded saying that.

Caiara looked slightly disappointed. "So, I wouldn't be able to buy things myself," she mumbled. "I was hoping to save up and buy a few things each month, sneak them into my room so Mum wouldn't notice."

"You're probably better off practising in the Library's lab until you get good enough. I sell some of my potions through

Wordarla's shop, and get a bit of money that way," Enkarini said. "Maybe you could sell your potions, once you're good enough, then you would be able to start getting your own equipment."

"That would take forever though." Caiara scowled at her small overnight bag for a moment before brightening. "Have we got time before your dad calls us for dinner? We could practise Seeing again if you want," she suggested.

Enkarini finished laying out the blankets and smiled. "Sure, dinner isn't until sunset. We've got a couple of hours yet," she said. "Maybe after Seeing I can set up some of my alchemy stuff and give you another lesson."

Caiara beamed. "Alright then. Let's get started," she said, settling down on a cushion. Enkarini sat opposite her, in her usual cross-legged position. "You want to try focusing on someone else this time, or keep trying your sister?"

"I'd rather keep trying to find Kandrina; I can't seem to concentrate on anyone else right now. Maybe when I know she's home and safe, I'll be able to See other people."

"Fair enough," Caiara replied. "You know the technique then, just close your eyes and relax."

Enkarini shut her eyes, almost casually picturing her sister's face. The vision took a while to appear, but she knew not to try and force it; unlike the magic Remlika had taught her, the harder she tried, the more difficult it got to See anything at all. She just held the image gently in her mind, recalling all she knew of her sister; the sound of her laugh, the twinkle in her blue eyes, the expensive perfume their father had bought her last year as a belated coming-of-age gift. After a few minutes, a vision flickered before her eyes.

It was similar to the last one, Kandrina and Remlik together in a forest clearing. This clearing seemed different, though; larger and with a trickling stream running through it instead of a pond. There was a strange, slightly distorted creature there with them, similar in appearance to the one she sometimes saw accompanying them. This one appeared to be talking to Remlik, though she couldn't hear much of what it was saying, just a faint whispering sound.

"We understand. Thank you for your patience," he said to it. The creature nodded sharply and disappeared, leaving them alone. Remlik turned to Kandrina and sighed heavily. "Well, we knew this was coming."

Kandrina frowned. "Why now? We're almost at the western edge, or so they say. Surely they can let us through a couple more glades; it would only take us a week or so."

"The leader reckons there is only one more glade between here and the west boundary and diverting to it would take longer than a straight run from here," Remlik explained. "The Mistress and the Tall One are busy tearing each other to bits in the eastern parts of the Forest, so hopefully they won't notice us until it's too late. We can stay here another two nights, get ready for the journey."

"I suppose we'll have to travel almost non-stop," she said softly. "I don't want to risk either of them catching up with us. We should be safe once we reach the desert, shouldn't we?"

Remlik dragged a hand through his hair, loosening several twigs and leaves. "I think 'safe' is a relative term here. I'm pretty sure the Tall One won't be able to touch us once we leave the Forest's boundaries, and from the sound of it the Mistress is a little preoccupied right now. We should be fine on those counts, but gods only know what lives out there."

To Enkarini's surprise, Kandrina actually smiled. "It's a desert, Remlik. The worst we'll have to contend with is a poisonous bug or two, and I think we can just step on those."

He tried to smile back, worry clear in his eyes. "I hope you're right." They both turned towards the stream, and the odd creature that she sometimes saw with them came bounding out of the trees. Remlik patted it on the head, welcoming it back as the vision faded out.

"What did you see? Is she okay?" Caiara's excited voice was the first thing Enkarini heard. "You were zoned out for quite a while there."

Enkarini rubbed at her ears; for some reason they were ringing quite loudly. "They're both fine, at least they seem to be. They're still in the Forest, but Kandrina said something about a desert," she said. "Remlik's worried, but he thinks they'll be safe from the devil and the red woman once they get to the desert."

The blonde girl looked puzzled. "Desert? I didn't think there was anything on the other side of the Forest."

"Nobody's ever got that far, so we don't really know," Enkarini pointed out. "There would have to be something though, eventually, even if it was just ocean. The world wouldn't just stop."

"I guess so." Caiara stared off into the distance for a moment, lost in her own thoughts. "Anyway, you want to try again?"

"Not for a while, my head's feeling a little sore now. How about we do some alchemy? I can help you mix a potion if you like," she offered. Caiara nodded eagerly, and they scrambled excitedly over to the corner where the alchemy equipment was stacked. Enkarini set up a small copper cauldron. "I'll show you how to mix a joy potion, it's the first thing I learnt to make."

The two girls huddled over the cauldron, Enkarini letting Caiara do most of the actual mixing. It was a fairly easy potion to make, only requiring half a dozen ingredients and an hour's brewing time, so there wasn't much for a novice alchemist to get wrong. By sunset, the batch had been mixed and cooled, and they were pouring doses into small flasks ready to go to Wordarla's shop.

"Girls, dinner's ready!" Harndak called up the stairs.

"We'll be down in a minute," Enkarini called back. "There, last one. I always leave a dose in the bottom of the cauldron, that way anything that hasn't quite dissolved settles there and isn't in the ones I sell," she told Caiara.

The older girl smiled. "Clever; and you get to keep some for yourself then too."

Enkarini smiled back. "I'll take these over to Wordarla's in the morning. You can come with me if you like, then Wordarla will know to keep the money for these aside for you."

Caiara stopped halfway down the stairs. "You'd let me have the money for them? We used your stuff, though," she said, surprised.

"Well, you did most of the work, so

you should get something for it. Joy potions always go quickly, so these will be sold in a few days." She staggered slightly down the last step, as Caiara had flung her arms around her and squeezed tightly. "Were you expecting me to sell them as mine?"

Caiara nodded, fiddling with her reddish-blonde hair awkwardly. "Thanks, Rini. You're a really good friend," she said.

Enkarini blushed, unsure how to respond. "Come on, Father's probably wondering where we are," she said, changing the subject.

"There you two are," Harndak said as they entered the kitchen. "We've got fish stew and boiled potatoes, and if you clean your plates there's some syrup cake for later. Oh, Enkarini, before I forget, you've got a letter. It looks like it's from Falp."

"Falp? Who's Falp?" Caiara asked.

"He's a boy I met when we stayed with the elves a couple of years ago," Enkarini replied. "We keep in touch; I haven't heard from him in a little while though."

"He's her boyfriend," Harndak whispered loudly.

Caiara smiled. "So, it's a love letter,"

she crowed. "I bet you can't wait to read that, Rini."

Enkarini hid her face, a little flustered by the teasing. "We're just friends," she exclaimed. She knew they were just playing around though and stuck her tongue out at Caiara when her father wasn't looking. Secretly, she was glad Falp had written to her. She wasn't really interested in boyfriends, but she did rather like the elf boy, and always enjoyed reading his letters.

~~~~~~~~~~~~~~~~~~~~

Semark faced his former advisor, now the Chief of Entamar, across the meeting table. As per the terms of their alliance, the Chiefs met once every four months to discuss matters and if needed, form a plan of action to deal with any issues. This was Semark's turn to host the meeting, and he'd had the Grand Hall prepared for its first important function in decades. Everything had been polished and dusted, there were staff on hand to provide food or drink if required, even the chair cushions had been freshly stuffed. Yet Satorus looked faintly uncomfortable, and Semark could not help thinking that something was amiss.

"How have you been finding the Chief's mantle?" he asked. Perhaps the mage was simply feeling overworked; he was new to this leadership business, after all.

Satorus shifted in his chair and cleared his throat. "More tedious than I had imagined. There seems a lot of mundane nonsense to deal with," he said softly. "I have been considering appointing a council to handle the day to day chores, so that I have more time for important tasks."

Semark gave him a wry smirk. "The minutiae can get rather overwhelming. I'd suggest you delegate to your assistant, but you're adamant you don't need one." He waved the subject away. "How is your plan to reinforce Entamar's border coming along?"

"Fairly well, the town's defences are stronger than they have been in decades. The wall is almost complete, and that Mistress lot are doing a fine job of keeping the townsfolk in line." He nodded, clearly satisfied with himself. "And Wirba? Have you had any further trouble with your siblings insisting you rejoin the union?"

"Not for a while now. I think they are focusing their attention on you and Entamar; Jindara in particular was highly concerned about the cult revival last time I heard from her." Semark poured himself a drink, more from a need to pause and collect his thoughts than any thirst. "I have been hearing some rumours about sacrifices myself. This, ah... it is all above board, of course?"

Satorus stared at him for a moment, his face a blank mask. "Don't concern yourself with that. I have the situation under control," he said softly.

A wave of calm passed over Semark. "That's fine then. What else was there... oh yes, Pokole. Has Devurak replied to our invitation yet? I have heard nothing and thought perhaps the letter had gone to you."

"Your brother is being very evasive," the mage growled. "He has declined joining our alliance, but given no reason, he refuses to say why he has sent labourers out to Yoscar, he danced around vagaries in his five-page letter without saying a single word of importance! How did you ever put up with the frustration?"

Semark laughed. "You think that's bad? I grew up with two of them, and Hinasi is ten times worse than Dev," he said. "If he doesn't want to give out information, he won't. Devurak is well practised in avoiding questions. We'll just have to find out another way."

A wicked grin spread across the mage's face. "Sounds like it's time to send my reconnaissance squad out again. Nothing better to spook someone than a fake attack preparation," he chuckled.

"Dev doesn't scare easily," Semark warned him. "It's uncanny how he can tell when something's amiss. He'll probably figure out what your squad's doing, and a way to hide whatever he's up to."

Satorus shot him a look of mock offence. "I'll have you know that nobody is better at devious plans than me. Except possibly my boy, but then he does take after me. Thank the gods," he muttered.

Semark raised an eyebrow but refrained from commenting. He had heard the rumours about Satorus' wife, Teadri, and seen for himself the woman's behaviour on his last visit to Entamar. It was hard to miss the semi-dressed, yelling drunkard stumbling through the streets at ungodly hours of the night. The mage rarely spoke of her, and this was the first time he had mentioned a son. Semark was curious but unwilling to pry; he knew Satorus valued his privacy highly.

"So, I shall send my loyal men to snoop around Yoscar and see what they can find," Satorus said. "With luck, we will find out what Devurak's secret building project is all about. I don't suppose you can think of anything it could be?"

"I have no clue, unfortunately. It is not a weapon, or new housing, or a temple of any kind, that would be obvious by now. Judging by the number of books we saw being taken out there, the only thing I can imagine is a huge library, but why would anyone build a library in the middle of uninhabited woods?" Semark pondered.

Satorus shrugged. "Who knows? Maybe your brother is planning to retire and seclude himself in a mountain of old tomes," he suggested. "Shall we adjourn for lunch? I am feeling rather peckish."

"Good idea." Semark stood, clicking

his fingers for a staff member to attend him. "Inform the kitchens that we require a meal. We shall await service in the dining hall." The two Chiefs left the meeting room, each of them content that their discussion had gone well.

~~~~~~~~~~~~~~~~~~~~~~~~~~~~~

"Will you stop elbowing me? We'll all have plenty of time to get in there," Enkarini hissed at the boy trying to push past her. When Glissia had told them yesterday that she would be opening Taliana's Archive this morning, all of the students had gotten excited. Since it was practically the only reason Enkarini was at the Inner Library, she had decided to get there early and wait, so that she could be one of the first ones in. Soris had been the only one there when she arrived just after sunrise, and slowly the others had joined them. The latecomers were stuck at the back of the crowd, and a few had tried to shove their way through to the front. Soris had made several back off with a shock a little too strong to just be static. Since their late-night encounter, Soris had not been quite so unpleasant to her, in fact he had almost been friendly, but was still rather cold and harsh to everyone else. She was beginning to understand why, though, and hoped to bring him round eventually.

Word filtered through the assembled students that the high priestess had arrived, and sure enough, Glissia appeared on the balcony moments later, along with Arikele and Disari. Everyone cleared a path for her, and she smiled at them. "Eager to study today, I see," she said. "The archive will be open until midday, Disari and Arikele will be supervising you. As always, no food or drinks; I can't believe I still have to remind you all of that," she said with a wink.

She unlocked the door, and the students scrambled through. "Be careful!" Arikele called, seeing a couple stumble in the rush. "Form a line, and proceed in an orderly fashion," she snapped. The librarian was strict, and rumoured to have a terrible temper, so none of the students wanted to annoy her.

After Arikele's warning, everyone seemed a little more restrained. Enkarini was third in, after Soris and an older man whose name she didn't know. She stepped into the room and stared around in awe. The place looked like a maze, made of rickety bookshelves and dusty old tomes piled high up to the ceiling. There were no windows, the only illumination came from dozens of hovering balls of light that floated gently around the shelves like miniature moons. Dust motes danced around in the draft from the door, and as the light caught them, they sparkled, making Enkarini think of fairies.

"Are you just going to stand there gawping?" Soris smirked at her. "Come on, the best books are over here," he said, leading her into the labyrinth of books.

She followed him between the shelves, past piles of scrolls, until he stopped beside one particularly old, tall shelf and crouched down. The bottom of this shelf was solid wood, about two feet high and three wide. Soris was prodding around one edge, and she wondered if there was a hidden drawer or something.

"Ah," he muttered after a few seconds, clicking something at the side. The front panel slid back, then down, revealing an opening just big enough to crawl into. "I found this last year. Get in, quick, before Arikele sees," he said, crawling into the shelf.

Enkarini hesitated. The shelf was quite large, but not enough to have room under it for both of them; not comfortably at any rate. How could either of them do anything squashed into there, anyway? She crouched and peered into the space, expecting to see a narrow gap with Soris squeezed into a corner. Instead, she found herself looking through the back of the shelf into a small, dim room. Curious, she crawled through.

As soon as she was out the other side, Soris clicked something and the front of the shelf slid back into place. "I always come in here when they open the Archive. Nobody else knows about it, so I can look up whatever I like without anyone breathing down my neck."

It seemed to be a tiny space, enclosed on all sides by the backs of shelves. A small, rickety table and patchwork chair sat in the middle; a dozen books spread across the table. There was a lone light ball floating around the ceiling, providing the room's only light. Soris stood by the chair, one hand on its back and the other held over the little bit of remaining floor space, muttering some incantation. With a small pop, an identical chair appeared in the space.

"Welcome to my personal study," he said grandly. "Take a seat and pick a book." He flung himself into the old chair, grabbed the nearest book and promptly buried himself in it.

Enkarini sat on the new chair and browsed through the remaining books. "It's really nice of you to show me this place," she commented.

Soris glanced at her over his book. "I figured I owed you something. You're the only one who kept trying, you know?" he mumbled awkwardly before hiding behind the tome again.

She smiled faintly; glad he was starting to trust her. She was sure there was a kind person lurking under the layers of scowling, sarcastic armour he had built up, and was determined to bring him out. She turned her full attention to the books; most seemed to deal with illusions and conjuring of various kinds, but one intrigued her. The title was 'Magick Most Complexe' and it had no author name that she could see. She opened it up and flicked through, unsure of what she was looking for.

"Good luck with that one," Soris chuckled. "I've had that in here for months, never been able to make any sense of it. I think it's what they call 'Wyld Magic', probably handed down from one of the Firsts."

She looked up at him. "Firsts?"

He snapped his book shut, rolling his eyes at her. "Hells, don't you know anything? The Firsts, the founders of the tribes, the mages who came here thousands of years ago and started our entire society? Didn't they teach you any of that in school?"

"I went to a temple school in Manak, Soris," she reminded him. "They didn't teach us anything other than gospel. So, tell me about these Firsts."

Soris sat up straighter, obviously about to give a lecture. "There were nine Firsts, who came to these lands from a distant place where magic was scorned. Each came from a different part of their homeland but joined together to find somewhere they could live in peace, where their gifts would be appreciated. Other mages came to them, tired of the persecution they had suffered, and assisted in creating a great gateway to a new land. This land was unspoiled and beautiful, and they claimed it as their new home. They carried their secrets with them and sealed the gateway so that none could follow and destroy their newfound harmony.

"The nine Firsts each had a different idea of how they should build their new society, and each formed a different tribe with their families and other, like-minded mages. The former librarian Bennett Wythe took a band of scholars and started the Bewein tribe. Alec and Rachel, the Meyer twins, would not be separated despite their differences and founded what would become known as the Akram tribe. The naturalist William Rabyn and others who felt connected to the earth formed the beginnings of the Wirba tribe. Paul Coltran, an adventurous sort, led the bravest among them south and founded the Pokole tribe, while the youngest First, Astrid Torver, headed towards the coast to be near the sea. Wealthy Enyeto Marsh began the Entamar tribe, taking his hoard and dreams of a glittering golden city to the east. Mark Napton, the oldest and most bitter towards others, led a small group north, which would become the Manak. Theresa Welldene, possibly the wisest of them, stayed near the gateway with those who remained, the beginnings of the Tewen tribe."

Enkarini was fascinated. It sounded like a fairy tale, but somehow it made sense. "How come they all had two names?" she asked.

"Where they came from, everyone had two names. A first name, which was like our names, and a last name, which was shared between all of their family members," Soris explained. "Some last names were just the head of the family's job, like Weaver or Potter, others were where the family came from, like Hill or Marsh. A few meant something in a different language. The Firsts decided that last names were unnecessary, because they wanted everyone to feel like part of one large family, so we don't have them anymore."

"Their first names were all so different, too," she said. "I mean, 'William' and 'Rachel' are such weird sounding names, aren't they? How did that change?"

Soris thought for a moment. "I'm not exactly sure, but I suppose it's got something to do with the language. Before all the mages separated into the tribes, they started developing their own language based on spells and incantations. Obviously not every word we say is a magic word, but they came up with words that were similar. I think it was so that if they were found by the non-magical people they'd left behind, the non-magical people would not understand them, think they only ever spoke in spells and would leave them alone."

Enkarini nodded thoughtfully. "So, you think this book might have belonged to one of the Firsts?" she asked, picking up 'Magick Most Complexe' again.

"Looking at how old it is, I'd say so. Nobody's been able to do Wyld Magic for centuries, since Taliana the Wise. I can hardly even understand what's written in there," he said.

She opened it at random and squinted at the tiny writing inside. It seemed to be written in a totally different language, which she guessed was from wherever the Firsts had come from. She could only understand a couple of words on each page and put it down after a few minutes. "I wonder if a translation spell would work," she mused.

Soris glanced at it. "I doubt it. The only translation spell I know is for spoken language, not written, and it only works for Old Elvish."

"What about the lizards' magic, though?" she asked. "Remlika brought back loads of books from the north, and she hasn't even got through some of them yet. Maybe there's something in one of those," she said.

He tapped the book he held against his chin, gazing thoughtfully into the mid distance. "I heard something about their magic being super advanced," he said. "Have you seen any of these books? Would you be able to bring any in here?"

"I can ask. If I can't bring them here, maybe you could come over some time and have a look through with me," Enkarini suggested. She looked down at the book she held. Something had drawn her to it, and she was determined to find out why. If she could translate it, she could at least find out if there were any spells in it to help her find her sister. "I'll talk to Remlika tonight."

~~~~~~~~~~~~~~~~~~~~~~

Braklarn sat cross-legged on the

library floor, surrounded by scrolls, maps and parchments covered in notes. He had been there much of the evening, arriving after Larinde was put to bed, and it was rapidly approaching midnight. Siale, the acolyte who worked there, had been trying to convince him to go home for an hour. She clearly wanted to close up and go to bed herself but could not leave while there was still someone in the library.

For his part, Braklarn was too engrossed to pay the girl much attention. He had finally come across a scroll, copied from an old explorer's journal, which had in turn copied from an ancient dwarven tome, that gave more details about the spiral gods and how they were linked. His conversation with the head watchman from Astator last week had only encouraged him to search harder for the answers. He reread his own parchment, where he had quickly jotted down what he knew for definite so far.

The dwarven god symbolised by the crossed-out spiral was referred to in the text as the Father of the Forest; his temples had been pulled down and forgotten about a thousand years ago. The Mistress had once been worshipped by the dwarves too, and her temples had been abandoned around the same time. The clockwise spiral, which the Butcher had carved into his victims and had been drawn on the sacrificial victim found near Astator, belonged to the Mistress' son, who had been known to cause 'mischief and strife' in the mortal realm.

The Church of the Mistress, as they were calling themselves, had not been behind the string of murders in Tewen and Bewein, but they had been doing their bloody work very openly in Entamar. They were probably working alongside Satorus, though he had not found proof of it, but there was another faction involved that was connected to the third spiral god, the Mistress' son. This third party had been behind the killings and had planted false acolytes within the Creator's temple to hide themselves. They were not openly linked with the Mistress cult but were using the fear and uncertainty that cult generated to further their own ends.

Braklarn stretched his neck briefly before turning back to his sprawl of scrolls. There had been something about the

Mistress' son in one of these books, he was sure... he pulled a tome towards himself at random and leafed through it. The information was in front of him, he just had to find it.

"Sir, are you quite certain you don't want my help getting these back on the shelves?" Siale's weary voice mumbled from behind him.

He glanced back at her. "Quite sure, thank you. If you want to go to bed, I can manage these by myself later," he told her. There was no real need for her to keep herself awake at this point; he'd been left to his own devices in libraries often enough.

She came around the side of his sprawl and perched on a chair. "I can't leave the books unattended. The high priestess would have my head," she said. "What are you doing with all this, anyway?"

"Finally getting close to the bottom of this mess," he replied. "I've been trying to work out this spiral god thing for over a year, and I think I've found the answers I need. I just can't quite piece it all together yet."

"Maybe I could help?" she suggested.

"Sometimes I find talking things over with someone else helps me work it out quicker."

In other words, she wanted to get him out of there so she could sleep. She was right though, having someone to bounce ideas off could be useful. "What do you know about the absent gods, Siale?" he asked. He needed someone who would at least have some clue what he was on about.

She shrugged. "My interest has always been in more practical knowledge, though I suppose I know a little more than most would be aware of," she told him. "Are you studying any particular absent god?"

"Three, though I suspect one is not really relevant. Last year, I was following up on the spiral symbols left on the victims of the Butcher; you must remember the panic everyone was in," he said. "I believed there was a connection to the Mistress and spent a lot of time chasing leads out in Entamar. A few months ago, I realised I had got the symbols mixed up, and had to start over with the whole triumvirate. I found this earlier this week," he pushed the scroll about the symbols towards her, "that sets out clearly which spiral belongs to which god.

The crossed out one symbolises an old dwarven god, which I don't think will have much to do with this. The other two belong to the Mistress, and her son. It doesn't say which god the son is to us, but I know he was worshipped by the People until after the merging."

Siale picked up the scroll and browsed it. "A habit of creating mischief and strife across the lands? There aren't many gods you could say that about," she mused quietly. "You think this third god is the one whose cult is behind the murders?"

He nodded slowly. "I have an idea of which god it is, but I can't find anything to confirm it. This is important; I don't want to go leaping to conclusions again." He paused, allowing several thoughts to click together. "Siale, if someone wanted to bring back one of the absent gods, and had little regard for how it might affect the People, how would they go about it? Hypothetically speaking," he asked.

She rubbed her eyes and leant forwards in the chair. "It would depend on which of the absent gods they wanted. If they were after Wirba's old god of trees, for instance, they would probably just need to plant some trees in his name and gather a few worshippers," she said tiredly. "The god of war would probably want a huge army gathered at his temple and several battles fought in his name before returning. In general, the more powerful the god was, the more you would need to do to bring them back."

Braklarn nodded slowly. "So, if, say, someone wanted to raise the god of chaos..."

"They would first need to be completely insane," Siale interrupted. "You are just supposing here, aren't you?"

"I'm trying to work something out," he replied. "I certainly wouldn't try to do this myself, but it's possible someone else is. I've got to find out who, and how to prevent them doing it."

Siale cast him a suspicious look. "I suppose if you were trying this yourself you wouldn't be talking about it so obviously," she mumbled. She stared down at her hands, lost in thought. "Rolar-Triak was a very powerful god. Anyone trying to bring him back would have to cause disruption and mayhem on a huge scale, probably throughout the whole of the People."

"You mentioned that to bring back an absent god you would need to gather worshippers, and perform whatever relevant acts in that god's name," Braklarn said. "I assume that would apply to anyone trying to bring Rolar-Triak back?" It was possibly an important factor; although there had been widespread disruption among the People the past few years, he had heard no mention of the old Chaos god. He had chased enough dead ends out in Entamar to risk another false lead here.

"I would assume so," she responded slowly. "Though it is entirely possible that a small number of worshippers could operate in secret, dedicating their actions to the god privately. Chaos is somewhat different from the others; from what I recall he would use deception and confusion to create mayhem, only revealing himself at the last moment. It is possible that someone trying to wake him could use the same methods."

Braklarn stared out of the window at the night sky, lost in contemplation. He could not shake the feeling that he was on to something here, but there were still too many missing pieces. The uncertainty and trouble surrounding the slow disintegration of the tribal union could possibly count towards bringing back the Chaos god, but he doubted it would be enough to fully achieve his return. Also, who would be crazy enough to even try it? Was there a connection to the Creator's temple, or was it a coincidence that the cult had put their false acolytes there?

"I don't think you're going to solve this one tonight, sir. Perhaps you should go and rest, come back tomorrow with a fresh eye," Siale suggested.

He looked around at her. "I suppose. It is getting late," he agreed. They gathered the scrolls and books, returning them to their respective shelves. "Say, I've been wondering for a while now; what happened to Kolena? I haven't seen her here for a couple of months now, has she moved to another library?" The older girl had been willing to let him stay all night from time to time, provided he put everything back before he left.

Siale shrugged. "I've no idea. The last time I saw her was about nine weeks ago, she told me she was going out for lunch and would be back in an hour. I didn't see her come back, but I was busy helping a young scholar with her studies that day and might have missed her."

Braklarn stopped dead in the middle of putting a book back. "That was around the last time I saw her too. She can't have been missing for nearly two months," he muttered. "Did she say where she was going, or who with, or anything?"

"I think she went with High Priest Gistran, but I've no idea where," Siale replied, looking worried. "You don't think something's happened to her, do you?"

"Gistran, as in the High Priest of Vrenid-Malchor?" Why was everything coming back to the Creator's temple? This had to mean something, there were too many connections. "Siale, was Kolena researching anything in particular the last time you spoke to her?"

The young acolyte shook her head. "Not that I know of, but she was quite involved with the tribal separation movement. Oh, and she did mention once that his Holiness was studying the absent gods rather intensely, and had asked for her assistance a few times," she said. "Perhaps he was doing the same as you, sir."

Braklarn nodded absently, and quickly returned the rest of the books. He bade Siale goodnight and headed home, wondering how these new pieces fit in. He would have to spend some time alone in his study to work this out.

Chapter Three:
New Skills

Remlika watched closely, taking note of how the girl did it. When she had been teaching Enkarini herself, the girl's bright emerald eyes had always been half closed in concentration, her otherwise pretty face scrunched up and silky brown hair scraped back into a rough ponytail so nothing could distract her from the focus needed for the spells. Now, she could see the sparkle in her eyes and her hair bounced around freely, as apparently there was no need to focus so intensely on the magic. Remlika had never been able to perform this kind of magic, in fact she had never even heard of half of it, but she was determined to attempt it later. From what Enkarini had said, the methods used in Higher Magic were completely different to the focused, approach of her own spells.

"So, there's no incantation, no hard

focus, just 'think and flick' as it were?" she asked when the girl had finished her demonstration. "That sounds more like the lizards' magic than what I was teaching you."

Enkarini shrugged and smiled. "It's a lot easier than keeping focus on something for ages. This way just feels natural to me."

"Whichever way you're doing it, I think it's very impressive. I am so proud of you," Harndak told her as he hugged her.

Remlika looked away with a small pang of sadness. There was one missing from that family, as there was one missing from her own life. Without Remlik, it seemed as though part of herself was gone. She had tried all she could think of, and she knew he was somewhere near the western edge of the Great Forest thanks to her own scrying and Enkarini's dreams but had been unable to find any way to get him home. She couldn't transport anything that far in one go, and from the little she had discovered about the Forest, it seemed that if she did manage to get out there and find him, she would have difficulty getting out again.

"I'd best go and check on supper,"

Harndak said, breaking from the hug. "Are you staying, Remlika? You're more than welcome, we have plenty to go around," he asked her.

She was about to decline – she had not forgotten Harndak's attitude towards her and her brother only a few years ago, though she appreciated that he was trying to make amends – but the thought of returning to the cold, empty house made her swallow her pride. "I'd love to. Do you need any help?"

"No, no, I've gotten rather good in the kitchen these last few months. Thank you for offering, though," he replied.

As he disappeared into the kitchen, Enkarini approached her. "Remlika, I've been wanting to ask you about the lizards' magic. You said it was similar to what I showed you earlier?"

She sat forwards on the sofa. "The method of casting seems similar, yes. Whether the actual magic is alike, I don't know yet. If it is, it could help mages like me understand Higher Magic better; Braklarn and I were able to work out some of the Li Buqu magic without too much difficulty," she mused.

"Can I take a look at some of the books you brought back?" the girl asked in a rush. "Only, I heard you saying something about translating spells in there, and there's this really old book in the Archive that me and Soris were looking at the other day, but it's written in a different language, so..."

Remlika looked up, frowning. "Soris? You're not associating with him, are you?" She was surprised that the girl would even look at him, after the way he had attacked her at the midwinter display last year.

Enkarini nodded. "He's not all that bad once you get to know him. Just kind of short tempered," she said. "So, about the lizard books; can I have a look? We just want to be able to translate this other book."

"Well... I was going to give some copies to the libraries anyway, but I wanted to work on them myself for a while first." Remlika tried to think of some excuse not to hand anything over; she had no real problem with Soris himself, other than the kid's attitude, but his father was bad news. She and several other mages she knew had been trying to keep the Li Buqu magic out of Satorus' hands for the past year, and letting his son get hold of their books was not the best way to do that. "How about I look through for a translation spell, and let you know if I find one?"

"But you don't know what it is we're trying to translate, what if you find a spell that won't work?" the girl asked. "Please let us have a look through ourselves, we won't misuse anything, I promise," she said earnestly.

Remlika sighed. She probably wasn't going to win this one, and since it was only a matter of time before the libraries started bugging her about giving them copies anyway, she gave in. "I'll make some copies tonight and we can take them in tomorrow. You'd better go and wash up for dinner, it smells like it's almost ready," she told her wearily.

"Thank you, Remlika!" Enkarini hugged her and ran upstairs to her room. She quickly washed her face and hands in the basin and pulled out her calling mirror. She had bought it from Wordarla's shop with the money from her potions, and most often used it to talk to Caiara. Tonight, she was calling Soris to tell him the good news.

The boy's pale face appeared, wearing a scowl. "This had better be important, I was just getting into bed."

"Remlika said she'll make copies of the lizard books and bring them to the Library tomorrow," Enkarini said in a rush. "We can start looking for a translation spell for Magick Most Complexe."

Soris' expression melted into a smile. "Brilliant! Next time Glissia opens the Archive, we'll be the only ones to read the First's book in centuries." He paused, a sly look creeping into his eyes. "Unless you don't want to wait for Glissia?"

Enkarini was puzzled. "What do you mean?"

"What if we could get into the Archive ourselves? There would be nobody to tell us time's up, nobody to disturb us, we could just do whatever we wanted, try out whatever we wanted, without interruptions," he said, a mischievous light dancing in his dark eyes.

She hesitated; as much as she wanted to know what was in that old book, she was uncertain about breaking rules and sneaking around to do it. "Maybe... I don't know."

Harndak shouted from downstairs, calling her for supper. "I've got to go, Father's doing supper. We can talk tomorrow," she said, about to put the mirror back.

"Ah, no we can't, I won't be at the Library again until next week," Soris told her. "Mother's taken ill, and since dad's too busy to look after her I'm stuck doing it. I'll see you probably Second Day next week," he said before ending the call.

~~~~~~~~~~~~~~~~~~~~~~~~

Jindara sighed heavily and rubbed at her eyes. She had enough problems of her own right now, with the tribal union in question and the remaining members clamouring for reforms, she did not need to have to deal with this as well. The odd, white parchment on her table had arrived yesterday, and she had not opened it yet. She knew it would be from Prince Michael, and she did not understand why he insisted on sending her these so often. At least once a month, she received a letter from him regarding possible trade and sending mages to the north. She had answered him already, told him that she would be happy to discuss trade once the People were in a more stable position, and whether any mages wanted to travel to his kingdom was down to the mages.

The thought occurred that this letter could be here because Tironde's grand ship had made it across the oceans, and he was letting her know they had arrived safely. With that in mind, she finally opened the envelope and read.

'Chief Jindara, I hope this letter finds you well. I am writing for several reasons, firstly to let you know that your youngest sister has contacted me from her ship. They are making good progress, according to her letter the mages on board have been assisting with the journey. She estimates that they are around three weeks sailing away from our shores, at the time of writing. When she arrives, I am sure she will send you a letter herself.

'I find I must mention trade once again, though I am certain you are tired of my pestering on the subject.' Jindara smiled at that. It sounded as though the Prince was as sick of writing these repetitive letters as she was of reading them. 'I had hoped the matter would be forgotten, with my father's death and our current troubles, but it seems my brother has taken up the subject along with the crown. Once things have settled down on both sides, perhaps we can arrange a meeting of delegations?

'This brings me to my next topic; I am wondering if we might be able to help you. I understand your tribes are going through some kind of political uncertainty, among other troubles. We have experienced our fair share of revolutions, upheavals and civil wars in the past; perhaps our history could help you, if only to give you some inspiration for a solution. If you so wish, I can arrange to send some relevant books to you for your perusal.

'To my final reason for writing; this may be a long shot, but have your people heard anything further about our dragons? The problems we are having right now may fall within their area of expertise, and their assistance is sorely needed. Of course, I understand if you can't help, but anything you may have found or heard would be appreciated.

'Warmest regards from Trizes, Prince Michael of Oakshire.'

Jindara stared at the letter for a moment. The writing looked rather messier and more rushed than his previous letters, especially in the last paragraph. She folded it up again and tapped the edge against her chin. Whatever was going on must be something major, otherwise Michael probably wouldn't have mentioned it. Could they be having trouble with the other dragons in their lands, perhaps?

She put it down and reached for some parchment to write her reply. She would thank him for the update on Tironde's ship; she had heard nothing from her sister since the goodbye letter. Her standard response to the trade question would do; she would ask Braklarn whether the offer of history texts would be useful before replying to that part. She had heard nothing about dragons since he and his people had left, but would promise him that if anything came up, she would let him know immediately. Her draft reply started, she rolled it up and slipped it into the drawer to finish later. She wanted to spend some time with Larinde before the evening meal.

"Focus on the sound of my voice, ignore everything else. You could close your eyes as well if you want, some find it helps," Andar suggested.

Enkarini let her eyes drift shut and pushed everything else to the back of her mind. She had asked Andar to teach her how to do mind contact with others, partly so she and Caiara could talk without Arikele telling them off, and partly because she wanted to see if she could use it to contact Kandrina. He had agreed, and while everyone else was at lunch they had found a quiet spot to start practising.

"Just concentrate on me, my voice, my thoughts. Keep your mind open, relaxed. Can you still hear me?"

"Yes, but it's like there's an echo. I'm hearing you twice," she told him.

Good. How about now?

She felt a small tickling sensation just inside her ears, and the echo had gone. "The echo's gone," she said.

That's because I've stopped speaking aloud. Try answering me without speaking this time. Think of what you want to say and push the thought towards me, he instructed.

So, is this how it works? We're actually doing mind contact now. She had thought it would be a lot harder than this, from what she had heard.

Andar chuckled. *Yes, we are. It won't always be this easy, though. I have had a lot of practice, and we are alone in a quiet room. When there's a lot of noise around, or a crowd of people, it gets harder to filter out the rest and contact the person you want. You'll also need to separate your own thoughts from the one you want to send out; I can hear everything you're thinking right now. Can you feel the connection? It's sort of a tight feeling towards the front of your head,* he asked.

She could feel something, like a sort of gentle pinch, but inside her head. *I think so.*

Right. So, imagine a wall inside your head, just before that feeling. Any thoughts you don't want me to hear, put behind the wall. Any thoughts you want to send to me, put in front of the wall.

She quickly did as she was told, imagining a big thick wall that hid her thoughts until she wanted to send one out.

How's that?

Much better, Andar replied. *I can teach you how to make a more effective mind shield another time, but that one does the job fine while you're learning.*

"There you are, I've been looking everywhere," someone called, disrupting Enkarini's concentration.

Andar turned and scowled at her. "We were in here because it was quiet," he huffed. "Enkarini wanted to learn mind contact, so we needed a secluded spot."

Caiara walked over to them. "Oh, that's brilliant. How are you doing with it? Are you finding it hard?"

"She was doing great until somebody interrupted us," Andar said pointedly.

Enkarini smiled. "It's fine. Can I try it with Cai? Just to see if I can do it with other people," she said.

"Sure. Caiara will have to initiate the connection though, I haven't taught you that part yet." Andar sat back to observe his new student.

Caiara knelt on the floor in front of Enkarini and smiled. After a few seconds, a warm tickly feeling spread over her, and she heard the older girl's voice. *So, what's up?*

Enkarini grinned at her friend. *This is amazing, I can't believe I'm doing it. Remlika's going to be so impressed when I tell her about this,* she thought.

Probably, Caiara replied. *Regular mages can't usually manage this sort of mind contact. They're used to focus and concentration being the only way they can access magic. This is much easier when you're relaxed and calm.*

"A'right y' three, I don't know what y' be doin' in 'ere but Arikele's lookin' f'r Andar. Somethin' about a book," came a high-pitched voice. Enkarini turned and saw Disari peering over at them from the doorway. "C'mon, she's waitin' in the library f'r y'. Y' girls better find somethin' quiet to be gettin' on with; she's in a foul mood f'r some reason," she warned them.

Andar grimaced and stood. "Well, this ought to be fun. We can carry on tomorrow," he told Enkarini as he followed the dwarf woman out of the room.

"I hope she's not in too bad a mood." Caiara stood. "Come on, JJ are waiting in the lounge." They practically ran across the hall, impatient to show off Enkarini's new skill to the twins. Jinna and Janna were sat by the fireplace, giggling over some silent joke one of them had told. Caiara waved at them. "Guess what Rini's been learning?" The twins glanced at each other before looking at Caiara, identical grins on their faces. "Hey, that's cheating!"

"What?" Enkarini asked. "What happened?"

Caiara rolled her eyes at the twins. "Andar already told them he was teaching you. I wanted to surprise them," she complained playfully.

Enkarini giggled. "Never mind. So, what are we doing today? Are we picking up our game? I think it was my turn to be the old crone next." Yesterday the four girls had stopped in the middle of a game. It was one they had invented together, and they made up new bits as they played.

One of the twins made a series of hand gestures, which Caiara interpreted. "They were talking about something they read in the Archive when we came in. A changing spell, or something," she said. "They were thinking of having different hair colours so that people can tell which one's which."

"That's easy. Jinna has a tiny freckle on her right cheek, and Janna has gold flecks in her eyes," someone said from a chair. He turned and leant over the arm. "Don't tell me you hadn't noticed."

Enkarini smiled; Soris really was observant to have noticed such little details. Caiara, however, frowned at him. "Didn't anyone teach you not to eavesdrop?" she asked acidly.

"Eavesdrop? You're talking so loud they can hear you in Astator," Soris retorted. "It's hardly eavesdropping when the person so obviously wants to be heard."

Caiara opened her mouth to reply, but Enkarini stood between them. "Hey, don't argue. It's neat how Soris notices stuff like that, isn't it? I hadn't realised it," she said in an attempt to calm things down.

The older girl seemed to struggle with something. "Well, I guess so. But he still shouldn't have been listening in."

"To our super top-secret conversation about changing hair colours. It doesn't matter, Cai," Enkarini said. "I'm sure he's

sorry for what he said, too. Right, Soris?"
She looked at him expectantly, and he
nodded slightly. "Good. You want to join
us? We're just chatting right now, but we
might play a game or something," she asked
him. This was the first day she'd seen him
here since their mirror call; maybe she'd get
a chance to talk with him about the lizard
books, and his idea of sneaking into the
Archive.

"Sure, I'd be welcome?" he replied
coldly, glancing at Caiara.

Enkarini nodded. "Of course." The
twins smiled and grabbed another cushion
from a pile nearby. Caiara wrinkled her nose
and started to say something, but Enkarini
nudged her. "Give him a chance. He's not as
bad as he seems," she whispered.

"He couldn't be worse, could he?"
Caiara muttered before dropping onto her
cushion. A small feather zoomed out the
side of it and into the fire, and the girl
watched it curl into ashes moodily.

Enkarini peered closely at the twins.
Soris was right; Jinna's tiny freckle was
almost invisible, but now she was looking,
the golden-yellow flecks in Janna's brown

eyes were obvious.

Playing spot the difference? came a sweet, musical voice.

She blinked, surprised. *Janna?*

I'm glad you're learning this. It gets lonely when almost nobody can speak with you, she said. *You seem like a good friend, Enkarini. We hope you'll be ours.*

Of course I will.

"Awkward silence. My favourite activity," Soris mumbled.

"No one's making you hang around," Caiara groused.

A look from the twins silenced both of them. *Caiara, be nice. We're all here for a reason. Don't judge Soris before you know him.*

Enkarini cast around for a topic to discuss before an argument began. "You know, there's something I've wondered about for a while now. Does anyone know anything about that room on the balcony? Not the Archive, the other door," she asked.

Jinna nudged her sister, and they started scribbling something on a bit of parchment. Caiara looked surprised. "It's probably a quiet room for the priestesses, so they can meditate or study or something. I said the first day you came here, remember?"

"That's what a lot of people think. I don't know if it's true," Soris said. "There are plenty of quiet meditation rooms and study rooms in the main temple, why would they need one in here?"

"That's what I was thinking. But if they're not studying or meditating in there, what are they doing?"

The twins put their hasty scribble down where the other three could read it. 'We think it's some kind of magic experiment. Sometimes when we've been here late, we've seen light flashing under the door and heard really weird noises. The doors always locked, but there's no keyhole; it has to be unlocked with a spell. We tried to hear what spell one of the priestesses used one time, but we couldn't quite hear the word properly.'

"That could be a possibility," Soris mumbled. "I wonder what spell they'd lock it with? The most common one I know of is *koghpek...* did it sound anything like *bat'sanel* when they unlocked it?" The twins shook their heads. "Must be another spell then."

"It could still be worth a try," Enkarini said. She had noticed Soris had a tendency to overthink things, when sometimes a simple answer could work just as well.

Caiara rolled her eyes. "You two aren't seriously going to waste your time on this, are you? It's probably nothing, maybe the priestesses just go in there to play games and unwind or something," she said.

"Well, if it's nothing, then it doesn't matter if we look into it or not, right?" Soris asked. "So, if it doesn't matter either way, why shouldn't we find out what's going on in there? If it really is nothing important, then it won't be a big deal. I can waste my time any way I like, and I don't know about Enkarini, but I want to do this."

Enkarini looked at Caiara, wanting to explain. "It's just that I'm curious. Why keep a room locked if there's nothing in there? Besides, if it turns out to be something boring then at least we'll know."

"It's the mystery making it exciting, I suppose," Caiara said. "I guess I'm sort of curious too. Okay. Let's try and find out what's in there. It'll make a change from studying, at least."

~~~~~~~~~~~~~~~~~~~~~~~~~~~~~

The temple was warm and full of the heavy, musky scent of incense. Braklarn tried not to sneeze, as the High Priest was wrapping up his morning service with a silent prayer. He had arrived early to see how Gistran conducted himself while performing his services and could not find any fault with him. His style was very different to that of the former high priest, but that was good. Gistran put far less emphasis on 'damnation and corrupting evil', instead talking about the glory of the gods, and their forgiveness of mortal mistakes. Braklarn did not frequent the Creator's temple, nor any other; the only god he ever paid attention to was Talri-Pekra, the knowledge goddess, and that only extended to the odd donation towards the libraries. The service concluded, and he waited for the congregation to file out before approaching the altar.

"Did you enjoy the service?" Gistran asked when he reached the front row of pews. "I felt this morning's hymn made a pleasant change. It feels good to sing the praises of the gods, does it not?"

Braklarn paused. "I suppose it does. Music has been missing from the temples for too long. It was the temple of Alch that began the practice of gospel singing, was it not?"

"I believe so. An intriguing sect, from what I have read. Did you know that the Sun Temple was open to the sky, so that the worshippers could better see their god? Though, one wonders what they did on rainy days," the priest said.

"I should think they got rather wet," Braklarn replied dryly. "Have you a moment to talk? I'm looking into the disappearance of an acolyte from the library, and since you have been studying there a lot lately, I wondered if perhaps you had seen or heard anything."

"Do you mean poor Kolena? She was always so helpful when I went to study; she had a knack of finding the exact book I needed." He turned to rearrange the flowers and candles on the altar. "I have noticed her absence lately but thought perhaps she had returned to Bewein. High Priestess Glissia has been recalling some of her best acolytes, so that they can take their vows and become fifth-circle priestesses. Kolena would certainly qualify," he suggested.

Braklarn thought about it. It was possible that she had simply moved to another town, or gone back to her mother temple to take her priestess vows, but if that was the case, she would have mentioned it to someone, surely? "I'd still like to check up on things. Nobody seems to know where she has gone, and I would have thought Siale at least would know if she was taking her vows."

Gistran shrugged, still facing the altar. "I'm afraid I can't speculate much further. The inner workings of the knowledge temple are as much a mystery to me as they are to any other man," he said. "I do hope nothing awful has happened to the young lady. She was a most promising acolyte."

Although the priest was saying all the right words, something seemed off in his tone. Braklarn thought he sounded almost amused, but that couldn't be right. "She was certainly very knowledgeable on several subjects. I understand she was helping with an in-depth study of the absent gods," he said.

"Yes, I was doing some research on the old religions. Kolena was kind enough to assist me," the priest replied softly. "She is very devoted to her work in the library; always willing to help anyone in need of guidance, and capable of finding the most obscure scrolls at times."

"I was asking about her at the library earlier, and Siale mentioned that the last time she saw Kolena was when she went for lunch with you, some weeks ago. Do you know what happened after that, where she might have gone?" Braklarn asked.

Gistran finally turned around to face him. "You want to know if anything happened while we were out?"

"I don't want to accuse anyone of anything, just trying to get a picture of what could have happened to her," Braklarn said softly. "Tracing her forwards from the last definite time someone saw her is the best way to do that."

"Of course, I understand and I'm happy to assist you in finding her," the priest replied. "We went to the Confused Duck for lunch, my sister Saleika runs the place and I try to send custom her way when I can. Kolena and I talked about various things; our studies, current events, the state of the world in general. She said she was a little short of funds, so I paid for the meal and we left the inn. I offered to walk her back to the library before returning here for the afternoon service, but she declined, and we parted. Now that I think of it, she did mention some meeting she had to attend," he said.

"Meeting with who, and where? Did she say?"

Gistran shook his head regretfully. "If she did, I'm afraid I cannot remember." A young acolyte appeared from a side door and beckoned him over. "It seems my duties call. I'm dreadfully sorry I couldn't be of more help. I will pray that you find her soon. May the gods be with you," he said before following the acolyte. The side door swung shut behind them, closing with a soft thump. Braklarn was about to leave – he had other things to attend to, after all – when he heard an odd noise coming from behind the altar.

Curious, he went to take a look.

There was nobody there, nothing that could be making the sound, yet he could still hear it. It was almost like someone laughing crazily, with some sort of droning chant in the background. He went closer and bent slightly to peer around the carved pillars, wondering if perhaps there was someone hiding in an alcove or in the small gap beneath the altar, and realised the sound was coming from beneath him. He knelt, pressing his ear to the stone floor, and heard a muffled crack, and the manic laughter stopped. The chant grew faint, as though the chanters were moving further away.

He knelt there for a second, mind racing. Could the sounds have been coming from under the temple? What was it Dekarem had said in that cryptic, panicked call? *'we're in the temple beneath the temple...'* what if he had meant a temple basement, where this cult had set up their pulpit? He scrabbled around, looking for a catch, a concealed handle, anything that might open a secret doorway, but found nothing.

The main doors of the hall opened,

and he quickly stood. He knew he had discovered something important here, he could feel it in his bones, but whatever it was would have to wait until the place was empty, and he could investigate in private. He left the temple, running through everything again in his mind. There were still pieces of this to be put together, but things were rapidly starting to fall into place in his mind. With luck, he was finally nearing some answers in this investigation.

~~~~~~~~~~~~~~~~~~~~~~~~~~

Enkarini sat quietly in her room. She was trying to See where her sister was, whether she had made it out of the Forest yet. The visions had been getting more difficult to reach, and she wondered why. Caiara thought it could be because the subject of her visions was further away, but Enkarini wondered if she might be reaching her limit with this particular skill.

She held her sister's image in her mind, thinking of the last vision she had seen. Then, Kandrina had been in a forest glade with Remlik, talking about their journey into a desert. Perhaps they had reached the desert by now, or would they still be trekking through the Forest?

After several minutes, the image of a shady clearing faded away, leaving Kandrina standing in bright light, looking out over a flat, yellowish expanse of fine sand. Remlik squinted up at the sky. "Looks around midday. It's going to be hot for a few hours," he said. "Should we wait here until it cools down, or make a start while we're fit?"

"I'd rather get going. We can always stop for a rest," Kandrina suggested.

They started walking, the Forest on their right, glaring sunlight and sand on their left, the creature trailing behind them. They had only gone a few paces when something rustled in the trees, making them leap away. The woman in red, looking far worse than she had in previous visions, emerged and glared at the three of them. She seemed to have been attacked; scratches marked her face and the dress was even more ragged than before.

"Just where do you think you're going?" she screamed at them. "There's nothing out there. You won't survive in that desert, you have nowhere to go! Come back in here and follow me, it's your only choice," she told them.

Kandrina stepped forwards to glare back at her. "Go back to the Hell you came from, bitch. I reject you, and your promises," she spat. Enkarini had never seen her sister look so furious before.

The red woman yelled and lunged forwards, out of the trees, but something caught her and held her back. It looked like a thick black vine, dragging her back into the Forest. Inch by inch, she was pulled shrieking back into the trees. When she had vanished from sight, the devil in black appeared at the edge of the Forest. He simply stood, watching Kandrina and Remlik for a moment, before nodding once and turning back into the trees.

Kandrina stood watching the shadows in the Forest for a while, her shoulders trembling. She let out an odd, choked sort of noise, and Remlik put his arms around her. "I want to go home," she wailed.

I'll bring you home, Kandrina. I don't know how, but I'll find a way, Enkarini thought to herself. Her sister had always seemed so strong, able to deal with anything, and she hated seeing her upset like this.

Kandrina started and looked around. "Enkarini?" Remlik looked at her with some concern. "I swear I just heard my sister, didn't you?"

"I didn't hear anything, Kandi," Remlik said gently. "Your sister's safe at home, back in Tewen, remember?"

"I know, but..." she looked around. "I'm sure I heard her. She said she would find a way to bring me home."

Remlik looked at her concernedly. "Maybe you're just missing her. We've both been through a lot, and that place hasn't helped," he nodded towards the Forest. "Let's take a break. I don't know about you, but this heat is getting to me already. There's a boulder over there we can hide behind, at least we'll have some shade."

The vision faded out as they reached the shadow of the rock, and Enkarini found herself shaking. How had Kandrina heard her? Had she accidentally made mind contact with her? Was it even possible over that distance? She slumped back against the side of her bed; her head full of questions.

At least they were safely away from the devil and the red woman, which was a relief. She could ask Andar about the mind contact thing next time she saw him at the Library.

Chapter Four:
Summoning

"I put them over there for the time being. Until I can review and categorise them, they'll be in the cupboard," Arikele said sharply. "And don't go thinking you can take them out, they're locked in there and will stay that way."

Enkarini started to protest – if it weren't for her asking Remlika to bring them, the books wouldn't even be here – but Soris pulled her away. "Right. Thanks for letting us know, we'll wait until they're on the shelves," he told the librarian.

"It could be weeks before she gets them out on the shelves, do you really want to wait that long?" she whispered furiously at him.

He threw her a look. "No, of course I don't. The idea was to find out where she was keeping them, not get her to hand them over," he replied. "Now we know, we can wait until she's busy with something and get into the cupboard ourselves. I can unlock it; you can grab the books since you know what they look like."

She nodded, realising what his plan was. He really was clever to think up things like that; she could never have come up with such an idea. They hung around the library for a while, browsing through at random, waiting for an opportunity. One arrived about mid-morning, when a young student somehow managed to make a shelf full of books topple onto himself. Arikele hurried over to him, clearly more concerned for her books than the student, and Soris headed for the cupboard in the corner.

He muttered a spell to unlock it, and the door swung open. "Quick, grab them before someone sees us."

Enkarini crouched to look into the cupboard. There were about fifty books in there, most that seemed to be old, tattered and falling apart. About a dozen of them were new and shiny, and these were the ones she took. Once she was out, Soris closed and relocked the door. "Let's go read them in the lounge. She'll notice if we start reading them in here," he said, leading her out of the library.

In a quiet corner of the lounge, Enkarini admired the binding on the books they had taken. They were covered in stiff green leather, polished to a shine and embossed with gold leaf. These were not the originals, Remlika had those under lock and key in her own study. These were the copies she had made, after translating them from the Li Buqu language into the People's. She opened the smallest one and started looking for a spell that could help her read 'Magick Most Complexe'.

Soris joined her, and discovered a list tucked into one book that told them certain types of spell were written together, and where the sections were in which book. This made it easier for them to find the likely spells and mark them for later. By sunset, they had found thirty-seven translation spells, some of which would probably be no good, but a few looked promising. "What do you think? Should we read up on these and try to figure out which one's more likely to work, or just try a few and see what happens?" Enkarini asked.

"You know what, they're just translation spells," Soris said. "It's not like we're messing about with anything dangerous, all they'll do is let us understand different languages. I say we try casting them all, that way we'll have the best chance at understanding the Firsts' language."

Enkarini felt a small twinge of uncertainty but cast it aside. "Let's do it." They gathered the books and made their way to the practice room, which was thankfully deserted since most people had left for the night. "I think there were some that we can't cast on ourselves; we'll have to cast on each other for those."

Soris was already flicking through the thickest book, which had a section full of language related magic. "Sure, we can do that. Here, these are ones we can self-cast. Might be better to practise with these, then if we make mistakes it's only on ourselves," he suggested.

"Good plan." She had never done magic like this before, so a little practice would be useful. After a few spells, she realised it was similar in a way to the illusion magic she had learnt; the spell

111

altered the recipient's perceptions, though in an aural sense rather than visual, so that the meaning of the word came through clearly in a language they could understand. "I think I've got the hang of it now. You want to try some of the other ones?"

"The ones we can't self-cast? Alright then. You want to do me first, or should I do you first?"

Enkarini shrugged. "Either way. I don't mind."

"Okay. I'll start," Soris said, pulling one of the books closer to him. "Here, this one's supposed to work for old texts."

About an hour later, the two of them left the practice room, their ears still buzzing and their heads spinning. "Well, at least one of those ought to work. Now we just need to get into the Archive," Soris said as they quietly returned the books to the library cupboard.

"You were saying something about not waiting for Glissia," Enkarini prompted. She had been wanting to ask him about that for a while, but never had a chance.

A sly look crept onto the boy's face. "I did, didn't I. See, I was thinking, what if I could get hold of the key? I've tried unlocking the Archive with magic, but it doesn't work; anyone who wants to get in needs the key, and Glissia has the only one," he explained. "So, if someone could copy it without her knowing, everyone would still think the Archive was secure, but we could go in there any time we wanted."

"Are you really suggesting we steal from the High Priestess?" Enkarini wasn't entirely sure that was a good idea. The Archive got opened fairly regularly, usually on Third Day and Sixth Day, so it wasn't as though they would have to wait long. She was about to say they should probably just wait, when Soris started talking again.

"Not stealing, exactly; not 'we' either. She'll still have her original key; I'm just saying I could borrow it long enough to make a copy. I've wanted my own access to the Archive for ages. If it can help you out too, that's a bonus. What do you say?"

Enkarini thought for a long moment. She didn't want to steal from anyone, least of all Glissia, but if she would still have the thing they wanted to take, it wasn't really stealing, she supposed. It would be nice to be able to get into the Archive when she wanted to, without everyone else flapping about in there... "Okay. When should we do it?"

Soris smirked. "Why wait? Let's do it tomorrow." The two of them arranged a time and went their separate ways.

~~~~~~~~~~~~~~~~~~~~

The temple was dark and silent. Sermons were over for the day, the worshippers had gone home, and Braklarn crept towards the front of the hall. For the last three days, he had been sneaking into the Creator's temple at night, to try and find an entrance to the basement, or catacombs, or whatever was below the building. The public parts of the temple had yielded nothing, though he had heard some odd sounds echoing from certain areas. Tonight, he planned to investigate the priests' rooms, at the back of the temple, to see if there was anything there.

He had tried to check up on Kolena from Gistran's story, but when he asked around the Confused Duck people had conflicting tales. Saleika had said the same thing as her brother. Some of the regular customers, however, had said they saw her faint at the table, and Gistran had carried her into a back room to recover. He was more inclined to believe the customers; he recognised Saleika as Dekarem's wife, who he had not known by name before, but knew to be an unfaithful and untrustworthy woman. He started to wonder if Dekarem's disappearance was linked to Kolena's and had begun poking around the temple.

After some subtle questioning, he had discovered that Gistran often held private meditation sessions with a certain group of acolytes. They all seemed to be fairly new acolytes, only with the temple for around a year and a half, and the others had mentioned that these 'special' acolytes were quite distant and reluctant to talk with their fellow devotees. He had not managed to speak with a 'special' acolyte at all; he suspected they went out of their way to avoid contact with anyone outside their little group.

Full of questions, and with nobody willing to answer them, he had spent the last three nights searching the temple for hidden rooms, concealed doors, even a furtive acolyte to follow. The priests' private rooms were the last place inside the temple he needed to check. He whispered an incantation that would help conceal him – it did not make him invisible but caused anyone looking at him to ignore his presence as long as he stayed still – and crept through the door into the priest quarters.

The narrow hall was dimly lit, lined with plain wooden doors on both sides. Braklarn peeked through the keyholes of each, only seeing the expected bed and set of drawers that furnished the simple rooms. Muffled snores echoed down the hall every so often, the only sounds to break the silence. He had reached the end of the corridor and was about to go home to start on a new plan, when he heard uneven footsteps behind him, as though someone was staggering, or being pulled along. Quickly, he backed up to the wall, freezing in place.

Someone was heading down the hall, for some reason only taking a few steps, stopping, then a few more steps. As the new arrival went past a candle, Braklarn could see it was a man, but before he got close enough to see any more detail, he turned into one of the rooms. Braklarn crept back, wondering if he was just stalking an acolyte who had snuck out to a tavern. Whoever it was had left the door ajar, and a low scraping sound came from within. He stood as close to the open door as he dared, looking through as best as he could without nudging it. The man was dragging the chest of drawers away from the wall, making just enough noise that Braklarn could ease the door open a little more without drawing attention.

Once the drawers were out of the way, the man leant on them briefly, wiping a hand across his forehead. He then stepped around them and seemed to draw something on the wall with his finger. One by one, the stones faded into nothingness, leaving a small hole just big enough for a grown man to crawl through. A blinding light shone from within and illuminated the man's face clearly.

Braklarn stood in shock for a moment; he had never expected stocky, well-fed Dekarem to look so haggard and thin. His hair, usually so meticulously shaved off, had grown through in clumps, some shorter than others. His face was drawn and grey-looking, his clothes hanging off him, but the worst thing was his eyes. There was no life behind them; it was like looking at a pair of shuttered windows.

Before he could shake himself out of it, Dekarem had crawled through the hole and it had sealed itself again. Mentally kicking himself for acting too late, Braklarn entered the room, shut the door, and knelt behind the drawers to look for a clue. If he had to guess, he would say that Dekarem had drawn the third spiral to open the wall. Was there a specific place it had to be drawn? Did anything else need to be done that he had perhaps missed? He decided he had nothing to lose, he had come this far and might as well try it and traced the symbol onto the wall a few times in different places.

Nothing changed on the wall but sounds started echoing in the corridor outside. A deep, resonating bell, and people shouting; he quickly stood and froze against the wall as the door to the room opened. A young, bearded acolyte poked his head in, looked around, and left. Braklarn caught the door before it closed again and snuck out.

He must have set off some kind of warning with his clumsy attempt to open the passage. As he left through the temple window, the same way he had got in, he decided to come back and wait in that room, every night if he had to, until someone opened the passage again.

~~~~~~~~~~~~~~~~~~~~~~~~~~~~~

The girl waited in the shadow of a pillar, watching the Library doors. She hoped the boy wouldn't be late, or worse tell anyone they had arranged to meet here. Disari had just left, locking the Library doors behind her. That wasn't a problem, since both Enkarini and Soris had keys, but the Archive would present some difficulties if Soris didn't manage to hold up his end of the arrangement. He was going to sneak into Glissia's private rooms and 'borrow' the Archive key, so that they could get in and take a closer look at 'Magick Most Complexe'.

She had transported herself home early and gone to bed at sunset, claiming that she was sleepy, then transported back to the Library after her father tucked her in. They were meeting at midnight, which should give them enough time to get in, take a good look at the book, and get out again before anyone realised what they were up to. As the temple bells rang out the midnight chimes, Soris crept around the corner and down the corridor. She snuck out from behind the pillar and met him by the Library doors.

"Did you get the key?" she whispered. This whole endeavour would be pointless if he hadn't.

"Of course, I got the key. You think I'd risk getting caught and not succeed?" he replied, waving the large, pewter key at her. "Let's get in there before someone catches us."

Enkarini unlocked the Library doors and pushed them open. The two of them waited for the doors to swing shut behind them before conjuring light balls. Though they were allowed into the Library at any time, they would rather not be seen trying to get into the Archive without permission. They tiptoed up the sweeping staircase and stood outside the Archive door for a moment. Everything was silent, their own nervous breathing the only sound in the hall.

Soris opened the door, and they

headed straight for the shelf room. Once they were inside, he conjured an extra light while Enkarini started looking through the book. It was a lot easier to understand now, though the words were ordered strangely. 'Take one of rose red flower powder grind, with water quart in bowl add, mix stir through until full mixed' was one line of instruction for a spell. As she read through a few pages, she realised that most of the spells in the book seemed to combine casting and basic alchemy, something she had not seen before.

"I've never heard of magic and alchemy being mixed like this before," she said quietly. "Have you, Soris?"

He stared at the page. "It's not done anymore, but I saw a spell like this in one of dad's old books once. He thinks that magic and alchemy were once more closely linked, part of each other and always studied together. Once it was discovered that pure alchemy could be used without magic, and pure magic without alchemy, the two got separated. This definitely means it's an incredibly old book; I might even be right about it belonging to a First," he whispered.

"Have a look at the front pages. Sometimes old books have the writer's name inside rather than on the cover."

Enkarini turned to the very front page of the book and flicked through the first few pages. Two were blank except some damp spots from age and a few squiggles that had faded beyond all legibility, but in the top corner of the third page there was a small, scribbled word. "Is that a W? Wyht... Wuhe..." she tried to decipher the cramped, smudged writing.

"Wythe, possibly," Soris said excitedly. "Maybe Bennett Wythe, or one of his family. I knew it!" He practically skipped around the small room, clapping his hands and laughing to himself.

She ignored him and went back to the main part of the book, where the spells were. The Firsts were interesting, but she had more important things to find in this book than the ancient, scrawled name of a long-dead mage. She flicked back and forth at random, waiting for a spell to catch her attention. 'Spell for Love'... no. 'Spell of Making Rain'... no. 'Dog Training with Magic'... definitely not. 'Spell of Calling'...

maybe? She paused in her flicking and read a few lines of the page.

'Three drops honey of stinging bee, add mix in water with twelve hopper wings … incant magic words of call to caster's familiar spirit … creature to guide help caster with many tasks …' *this looks good,* she thought. *Maybe it will call something to help me find Kandrina.* She reached for a quill and piece of parchment to copy the spell onto, but Soris stopped her.

"I know a better way," he said. He held one hand over the book, the other over the blank parchment, and mumbled the same incantation he had used to duplicate the chair before. After a few minutes, the spell from the book had copied itself exactly onto the blank sheet. "Much quicker. So, you got what you were after?"

Enkarini nodded. "I think so. If it doesn't work, I suppose I can come look for something else," she said. She didn't even know what had drawn her to the old book in the first place. Sometimes it was best to just let her feelings take over instead of always second-guessing herself. They left the Archive, and she started down the stairs.

"Hey, while we're here," Soris started, pulling her back up. "Let's take a look at this mystery door. Nobody's around to tell us off right now."

She followed him across the balcony reluctantly; they would be in enough trouble if someone found out they were sneaking around the Archive, she dreaded to think what would happen if they were caught trying to get into the locked room in the dead of night. When she had agreed to try and find out what was in there, she'd imagined they would just be asking questions and nosing around while the Library was open, not trying to break in at midnight.

Soris stood in front of the door for a moment, peering closely at it. "I can't see any obvious wards or anything. Maybe a basic unlock spell..." he muttered a few different words, but none of them worked. "You know any others we can try?"

"Nothing you haven't just tried," Enkarini said. She stifled a yawn. "Can we maybe do this tomorrow? I'm kind of tired."

He either didn't hear or ignored her. "The twins reckon there's no key, I can't see a keyhole, but maybe there's a different kind of key? Some kinds of ore have unusual properties, they react with metals and things, maybe it's something like that." He ran a hand around the smooth metal handle, over the heavy wood of the door and the frame. "Any ideas?"

Enkarini walked up to the door and tugged on the handle. "Well, someone might have forgotten to lock it," she said defensively when Soris started snickering. She took a piece of parchment from her pocket, folded it until it was firm and tried to run it around the edge of the door. "I saw my brother do this once, when he got locked out one night. He managed to wiggle the bolt open somehow."

"Did 'e now?" someone called from the ground floor. "N' I s'pose y' be tryin' to copy this brother o' y'rs?"

They jumped and turned to see Disari rapidly mounting the stairs. "Erm, we were just..." Soris began.

"Y' were just what, wantin' to see the what the 'Igh Priestess does in 'er private rooms? Tis none o' y'r concern what be goin' on in there. A matter f'r only them

with experience n' wisdom to deal with."
She chivvied them away from the door and
down the other side of the balcony. "Now,
y' be off to y'r beds, young'uns. N' I'll be
'avin a word with Priestess Glissia about
this in the mornin'," she told them as she
shut the Library doors.

They turned to face each other. "Well,
now we know it's more than just a quiet
study room," said Soris. "If it wasn't
something important then she wouldn't have
been in such a hurry to get us away."

"I guess so," Enkarini yawned. "I'm
going to head home and sleep. We can
worry about the room later; I want to try out
this spell first." They agreed to meet up
again the next night to cast the Spell of
Calling and headed for their homes.

~~~~~~~~~~~~~~~~~~~~~~~~~~~~~

The following evening, Enkarini
transported herself and Soris out to the
plains, far from the People's towns, just in
case anything went wrong. She had told her
father she was staying the night with Caiara
so that he wouldn't worry. She had no idea
what Soris had told his parents, but
suspected they were too busy to be

concerned with where he was.

"You sure you wanna do this, kid? You don't know what you'll end up summoning," he said.

"Yes, I'm sure. And don't call me kid, I'm only four years younger than you," she told him. Sometimes she didn't know why she bothered hanging around with him. "It doesn't look like that difficult a spell. Or potion. What would you call this?" Like most of the old book, the spell she had found was a bizarre mixture of incantation and alchemy.

Soris shrugged, staring off into the distance. "Old Magic. Wyld Magic. Higher Magic. Pick a name, there are tons in the old books." He looked back at her. "I still don't think you'll be able to make this work. I've been studying magic for years, and never been able to..."

"Hand me the waterskin," she interrupted. She had heard about how Soris was better than her at normal magic far too often. She transformed a nearby rock into a small cauldron and lit a fire under it. Soris handed her the ingredients as she asked for them, and she carefully brewed the 'Essence of Calling' as the book called it. As she added the herbs, insects and other odd things she preferred not to think about, she spoke the words of the spell that accompanied it.

After a couple of hours brewing, the potion was ready and simmering gently. "Right. Now it says in here that the spell will summon 'that creature which is closest to the caster's spirit'... what does that mean?" Enkarini asked.

"Probably you'll end up with something tiny, fluffy and useless," Soris mumbled. "Just cast the damn spell and find out."

She threw him a withering look before beginning the spell. She checked the old book several times to make sure she got it right. If this could help get her sister home, she really didn't want to mess up. First, she created a protective circle around herself and Soris. Next, she poured small amounts of the potion at each of the cardinal points. She took a moment to focus on her desire – to call a familiar that would help bring her sister home – and chanted the words in the book. "*Na kirawo, na gayyato, na kirãyi zuwa gare ka. Ruhu, ta zo gare ni!*"

For a moment, nothing happened. "Wow. That was dramatic," Soris said.

Just as she turned to glare at him, a sound like leather flapping in the wind came from overhead. Both of them looked up, and saw a huge shadow flying above them. Enkarini's first thought was to run, but she knew the circle she had cast would keep out anything that intended harm. Her legs shaking, she watched the shadow circle lower until it landed on the plains, a huge black creature with glittering gold eyes. It was the size of a house, with a great pair of wings that it folded on its back, and its skin was covered in shining black scales that almost sparkled in the moonlight.

"Speak thy name, young sorceress," it said in a deep, rumbling voice.

"Um... Enkarini," she stammered eventually. "How... what... who are you?" she asked.

The creature lowered its head. "I am Maldor, Shadow Dragon of the North. I have come in answer to thine summons." It straightened up and looked at her curiously. "Thou didst summon me by the ancient Spell of Calling, didst thou not?"

"I, um, I guess so. I did cast the spell," she said. She couldn't help glancing sideways at Soris and mouthing 'tiny, fluffy and useless?' The boy cringed.

"Thy purpose in calling me?" asked Maldor.

Enkarini looked up at the great black dragon. "I need help. My sister is trapped in a desert beyond the Forest of the West, being hunted by a devil. I want to go and help her escape. Her friend, too," she added, recalling at the last minute that Remlik was there with her.

Maldor seemed to think about it for a moment. "There are a few ways I could assist thee. How soon wouldst thou want thy sister home?"

"As soon as I can find her," Enkarini replied. She had waited far too long to see Kandrina again.

"Then the easiest way by far would be to go and fetch her." The dragon lowered himself to the ground. "I shall fly thee to find thy lost sister."

Hardly able to believe what was happening, Enkarini climbed carefully onto the dragon's broad, scaly back. She looked down at Soris expectantly, assuming he would want to be part of this.

"Oh, Hells no," he exclaimed, frantically shaking his head. "You go, I'm not getting up there. I'll cover for you back in Bewein," he offered.

Enkarini nodded gratefully. "Thanks, Soris. I'll be back soon." She hoped so, anyway.

Maldor straightened up and unfurled his wings. "Hold tightly, young one." The girl found some purchase on the ridged scales in front of her and held fast.

The dragon leapt into the air, eliciting a yelp of shock from Soris and a whoop of excitement from Enkarini. She had never experienced such a thrill, and for a moment she completely forgot about her sister. They wheeled about in the air, Enkarini catching a last glimpse of Soris gawking up at her, and they were off. Maldor flew at such speed, they were across the plains and approaching the dwarven lands within a couple of hours. Enkarini stared down at the twinkling lights of Little Graston as they flew over it. It had seemed to be a big place when she and her father had stayed there, but from this height it looked like a minute clump of candles in the dark.

"It will take some time to reach the Forest, Enkarini," said Maldor. "I expect we shall be at the edge of the trees by sun-up. If thou wouldst rest, I will use my arts to ensure thy safety."

"Your arts?" she asked, surprised. "You mean you can do magic too?"

Maldor chuckled. "I can indeed, though it is unlike that which thy people know as magic. I suspect thy Wyld Magic is the closest to ours."

Enkarini had about a thousand questions but decided they could wait until morning. Her eyelids were feeling very heavy. "Would you wake me up when we get to the Forest?"

"Of course, young one. Sleep, I shall wake thee at sunrise."

She slid down a little into a small dip in the dragon's scales and curled up to sleep. Part of her wondered if she had actually fallen asleep in the Library, and this whole thing was some fantastic dream. She supposed she would find out when she awoke.

~~~~~~~~~~~~~~~~~~~~~~~~~~~~~~~~~

Jindara sat before the window in her private room, going through the final draft of her proposal for the reforms. She thought she had everything covered, but as the meeting was tomorrow, she just wanted to double check. Garren, Hinasi and Onkadal were all bringing their own ideas, and the four of them would hopefully be able to reach some agreement that worked for everyone. She had gone over one proposal already, read it out for Braklarn, and torn it up when he reminded her that she was meant to be focusing on Tewen's needs, not making plans for every town and village.

This one was better, more concentrated, and she told herself repeatedly that she had not neglected anyone, the other towns were making their own plans. Finally, she laid down the parchment and stretched her arms out in front of her. *If I've forgotten anything at this point, it's probably not that important,* she told herself.

She had just closed her eyes for a second when a flash of light burned through her eyelids. She sat up, staring out of the window, wondering how the cloudless sky had produced lightning.

"Chief Jindara," came a sibilant voice from behind her. She spun round, and immediately yelled for her husband as she seized the letter opener from the desk.

Somehow, one of the Li Buqu from the north had broken through the protective wards erected after the Lizard War and was eyeing Jindara closely. "What are you doing here, snake?" she demanded. The last she had heard of them; their leaders had decided to leave the People and their lands alone.

It cast an amused glance at her makeshift weapon. "Such a tiny blade would have little effect against me, were I here to cause harm."

"You think you're important, I suppose," Jindara taunted. "What are you, the advance guard?"

"I am Xhih'a, Piraj of the Li Buqu," it answered coolly.

Braklarn burst into the room, obviously concerned by Jindara's unexpected shouts, and immediately conjured a handful of frost on seeing the lizard.

It almost smiled. "You realise that if I

had come here to attack, she would have been dead before you entered the room," it pointed out. "Nor would I have announced my presence to you," it told Jindara.

"Then why are you here?" Jindara asked again.

"To deliver a warning. The Lokres do not agree with me, however, I believe your people ought to know of the danger that may be approaching," it hissed. "For the last year, we have been scouting the far north, over the mountains you may know as the Grey Peaks. We assumed, incorrectly, that the area was uninhabited."

Jindara suddenly remembered where she had heard the name 'Grey Peaks' before; during her conversation with Prince Michael at the end of the war, when he had explained how and why he had ended up in the People's lands, he had mentioned his search for the green dragons from his own lands. "Let me guess, your lot pissed off the crazy dragons that live there and now you're running scared," she said, glaring at the lizard.

Xhih'a looked affronted. "We are not 'running scared'. I have personally seen to the defence of our lands from these beasts," she proclaimed. "The creatures are flying south; they may grow weary and return to their eyries before reaching your lands, but they may not. I suggest you form your own defences in preparation."

"And we should listen to you because...?" Jindara was not about to take orders from a former enemy, especially not the ones who had killed her father. "For all I know, this is some plot of your people to try and conquer us again! Make sure we're distracted with nonsense, and invade while we're looking the other way," she cried.

The lizard mage bared her fangs, her expression one of clear contempt. "Whether you heed my warning or not is down to you. Believe me, if we wanted to conquer you, we would do so, without any need for distractions." She vanished in another flash of light, leaving both Jindara and her husband stunned.

"What was that all about?" Braklarn mused. "I thought we'd seen the last of them two years ago."

"It would seem not. What do you make of that pretty story?" Jindara asked him.

He let his handful of ice melt, dripping onto the rug. "I've no idea. Prince Michael did say something about their green dragons living up in the mountains, and I seem to remember Remlika mentioned that she'd heard them talking about expanding north rather than south. The lizard could have been telling the truth."

"Or it could be some sort of ploy, or even their idea of a practical joke. We never could fathom the way those creatures think," Jindara pointed out. She frowned heavily, thinking of possible courses of action. "Let's assume for a moment that it is true. What would we need to do to protect ourselves... obviously prepare the armies for battle, find some way of protecting the towns," she muttered to herself. "But how? We've never come up against something like this before, and the records from the last dragon attack are more myth than fact."

"Write to Prince Michael," Braklarn suggested. "He seemed to know a lot about dragons. Maybe he'll have some advice for how to defend ourselves. He did ask you to let him know if you heard anything about them in his last letter, anyway."

Jindara looked over at her husband. She had missed him the last few weeks, with his investigation and her reform plan taking up so much of their time, but he always managed to come through for her when she needed him the most. "Good idea. In the meantime, I will have the army start drills for aerial attacks, and let my siblings know about the potential threat."

Braklarn came over and took her hand. "Why not take a short break," he said softly. "It's well past midday, and Larinde is getting rather tired of pulling daddy's hair. Come and spend some time with us."

She smiled and followed him to their quarters, grateful for the excuse to stop working and play with her young daughter for a while. With both herself and Braklarn so busy these days, who knew when the three of them would have another uninterrupted moment together?

Chapter Five:
Fight and Flight

"We have reached the Forest, young one."

Enkarini stirred, briefly wondering why her father sounded so different this morning, before she recalled what she had done the night before. She sat up carefully, marvelling again at the view around her. The sky was just beginning to brighten, casting long shadows across the ground. She hoped the shadows from the dawn light were the only reason the mass of trees beneath them looked so dark and forbidding. "How long will it take to get across? I'm pretty sure my sister is on the other side, in a sort of desert."

"It will take some hours yet; there is some form of shield over this place, so I must travel at a slower pace than I usually would." They flew in silence for a while, the trees sliding under them, uniform and almost black. "Dost thou have questions, Enkarini? We have plenty of time to speak," he said.

The things she had wanted to ask last night came rushing back, and it was hard to pick just one to ask first. "Last night, you said our Wyld Magic was closest to your kind of magic; what did you mean?"

"Precisely that. Thine ancestors, on leaving their birth lands in search of pastures new, took all human magic with them. At the time, the only magic practised was that gifted to thy race by my own; the Elders taught humans how to use magic long ago, and until the Exodus human casting remained similar to the original methods. Once thy Firsts reached these lands, changes began; material manipulation – which thou knowest as alchemy – became separated from energy manipulation. As the ability to control magic slowly grew diluted, thy mages found new ways to call upon the energy. Wyld Magic was lost, and the art lessened for it."

"So…wait, my ancestors? Do you mean I'm descended from one of the Firsts?" she asked, getting excited at the thought.

"All thy People are, distantly. Humans did not live on this landmass until their arrival," Maldor told her. "Almost every mage on Trizes left in the Exodus, taking magical ability with them. It is rare that one is born with the gift there now. We teach those few that do develop it, as humans there have lost all knowledge of magic."

"Why is that? How come people – I mean humans – can't do magic there?"

Maldor took some time to answer. "Magic is an inherent property of this world; the energy of it seeps from the very rocks. We believe that the ability to access that energy is inherited, that is, passed down through generations. Some have a strong ability, others weak, and some cannot perform magic at all, but pass the capability on to their own children."

Enkarini paused, thinking over what she had heard. She didn't know where Trizes was, but she thought the name sounded familiar. "So, we originally came here from this Trizes place, and only people who could do magic came?"

"That is correct. I believe there were a handful who could not; the partners of mages, a few close friends, but most were able to cast." A roar below them interrupted the conversation. Smoke was rising from a point ahead, trees swaying and thrashing as though in a high wind, but there was no wind to speak of. Maldor banked to go around the plume of black smoke.

As they passed near the centre of the disturbance, Enkarini looked down, wondering what could be making such a noise, and instantly recognised the beings from her dreams. The tall devil in black was fighting with the woman in red, the trees seeming to bend and twist at his gestures, tongues of flame leaping from her tattered dress to devour the branches. "Wait, I know those two! They were keeping my sister here!" she cried.

Maldor slowed, circling over the fight. "We ought to continue onwards, young one. This is not our battle, and it would be foolish to interfere," the dragon said. At that moment, the woman in red looked upwards and spotted them. She shrieked a curse, and her flaming dress seemed to reach up towards them, causing Maldor to swerve to avoid it. He dropped lower and shuddered as though he had hit something. "Though it seems we now have little option. Ready thy magic, young one."

The dragon swooped down through the trees, scattering needles and twigs, a stream of black flames issuing from his mouth. Enkarini tried to think of any defensive spells she could, but what had she learnt? Remlika had never taught her much battle magic, and since being accepted into the Library she had been too busy working on other things. She called up a freezing spell, thinking that it would at least be of use against the woman's fire, and cast it down at her.

The red woman stumbled slightly as the ice spell hit her, and she peered upwards. "You?" she said, almost delighted. "This worked out well; I wanted your sister, but you share the line too. My temple will rise again!" She cackled madly, and almost flew into the air towards them.

Maldor swept his tail at her, knocking her away, and a thick black rope appeared to drag her backwards. Enkarini followed the rope with her eyes, wondering where it had come from, and realised it had somehow sprung from the devil. "Get us out of here!" she shouted, hoping Maldor could fly away while the woman fought off the devil. He turned awkwardly in the confined space, flew up towards the treetops and sped away down a path. "Can't you fly us above the trees again?" she asked, glancing behind nervously.

"I cannot, Enkarini. The shield over this place is too powerful," he said. He flew through the trees, his wings skimming the branches on either side.

She suddenly realised what had happened; when he dodged the woman's fire, he had entered the shield spell he had mentioned, and they were now trapped like Kandrina had been. "But how did we end up in here if this shield thing is so strong?"

"It appears to allow entry, but not exit. We shall have to find a way through the spell. There are always weak spots in spells this vast; together we should be able to locate one." He stopped, hovering over the path, glaring ahead. Enkarini leant around the side of his neck to see what the problem was.

The devil stood in the path, leaning

against a tree. "I knew you would be something special," he said, his eyes wandering over them both. "I had no idea just how special, though." Behind them, the woman screamed in fury. "Unless you wish to be forced into serving my sister, I suggest you follow me."

Enkarini saw little choice; so far he had done nothing to cause them grief, while the red woman had attacked fiercely. She asked Maldor to follow him, but keep at a distance, so they could escape if necessary. She had no idea what was going on here and did not want to trust him after the way she had seen him torment her sister, but at least he wasn't throwing fire at them... yet.

The doors of the hall were propped open, in hopes of tempting a passing breeze into the stifling room. Jindara had a large pitcher of ice-laden water by her side, as did the others. The heat was such that even Hinasi had foregone her usual embroidered gowns and worn a light blouse instead. Onkadal lay spread-eagled over his chair, sweat pouring down his face. Garren was the only one who appeared moderately comfortable, but even his face was shining with perspiration and turning redder by the second.

"Shall we begin?" Jindara said, trying to resist the temptation to pour the ice water over her head. "We have all had a chance to read each other's plans, I for one believe that they can be enacted without too much difficulty."

"They can, that's for sure. The question is whether they will be enacted without difficulty," Onkadal said. "I still think we should just go ahead with this. Waiting for everyone else to get involved and debate over it could take months."

"That is rather the point, though. The whole reason people have been kicking up a stink about separation is because they are tired of decisions being made for them. The People should have a say in these reforms," Hinasi pointed out wearily. She and Jindara had gone over this repeatedly with him, and they were both sick of making the same points all the time. "Our individual plans for our towns seem just fine; I would like to raise a query about the future of the union, though. The idea when it was formed was that the tribes would come together and act as one tribe under a single Chief, but now we will be going our own ways, so where does this leave us?"

Jindara rolled her glass across her forehead, savouring the coolness against her skin. "We are effectively planning the dissolution of the union as we know it. If each town is to have its own laws and its own Chief, perhaps an alliance would be a better way to describe it? We will, I hope, remain on friendly terms with each other, after all."

"Astator certainly intends to," Garren chimed in. "As I have said before, the union as it stands is no longer fit to serve the People's needs. We have plans in place for dealing with any external trouble should it arise, but otherwise will be independent from one another... yes, I think an alliance is the way to go. The majority of the public should be at least content with that."

"It also allows much more room for other tribes to join – or rejoin – at a later date, without going through so many changes to conform to what the rest are doing," Hinasi said.

Jindara looked across to her brother, who had slumped even further down into his chair. "Onkadal? Have you any input here?"

He pushed himself more upright. "It sounds like a good plan. Cooperation and trade, but without handing over control to anyone else. I'm in," he said sluggishly. "Right now, I just want this damned heatwave to sod off."

"I think that's one thing we can all agree on," Garren chuckled.

"Let's put that in the reform plans then," Jindara said. "The alliance idea, not the heatwave." They each made a note at the end of their plans, so that their respective townspeople would know what was going on. "Hinasi, you mentioned in your last letter that Devurak had been in touch about what he's doing out in Yoscar; care to elaborate?"

"Actually, before we move on to other topics, might I raise an issue?" Garren asked. "As I'm sure you all know, Astator has recently returned to its previous system of electing a Chief. I was wondering if this could be something to introduce on a wider scale? Of course, your own tribes had their own methods once as well; perhaps you would prefer to return to those," he said.

Jindara nodded slowly. "It could be worth a discussion, certainly. Some way of choosing a leader other than inheritance would be good, otherwise there could be several problems in the future; with the exception of yourself, we are all siblings, so our descendants could potentially try to claim Chieftaincy of more than one tribe."

"Akram's former way of picking a Chief was by rule of the sword," Onkadal said. "I could see that making a comeback."

Hinasi frowned into her glass of water. "Bewein chose a council of seven as leaders, the most educated and intelligent in the tribe. I don't know whether that would work now; so many of our fine minds tend to leave us to expand their field of study."

Jindara was sure the two of them were thinking of ways they could hold on to their places at the top. She had little love for the Chief's mantle; she had taken it as a matter of duty, rather than ambition. "I can't quite recall how Tewen chose a leader, I would have to look it up. Letting the citizens decide would be a fair way of doing things, though." After a moment's thought, she pulled her plan closer. "I shall ask whether it would be something the people of Tewen want."

A few moments passed in silence, each of them lost in their thoughts, before Jindara remembered she was going to ask about Devurak. "So, as I was saying; you heard something from our brother about his plans out in Yoscar?" she reminded Hinasi.

"Yes, he sent a letter explaining most of what he's doing out there. I'll read it out, much easier than passing it around to you all," Hinasi said. She pulled a small scroll from her pocket and cleared her throat. "Dear siblings, I hope this letter finds you well. I feel it is time to let you all in on my plans, at least to some extent. You may have heard that I have been building something in the old village of Yoscar; this is correct, though the rumours that have reached me are laughable. I am in fact working on a grand place of learning, something called a university, where I hope the greatest minds among the People will gather to study and teach.

"This is no mean undertaking and has

involved much planning and work. I believe I have gathered an almost complete library of texts known to the People, thanks to the hard work and endless research of very patient scholars. The old village, which had fallen so far into disrepair that it was little more than a handful of ruins when we arrived, has been restored and expanded to serve as accommodation for students and teachers. The new buildings are almost complete, and ready to receive classes of young scholars.

"You may be wondering where this idea came from; I have long thought that the People needed a place of unfettered learning, where ideas are allowed to flow freely rather than being hidden and controlled by various factions. As I am certain you will remember from your history, Yoscar was originally intended to be such a place, a haven for scholars, but circumstances prevented its completion. I have been quietly restoring the old village for some years, but I must admit to being a little unsure of the best way to do this until recently. When young Prince Michael contacted me, he mentioned a university in his own lands, which seemed like an ideal model for my own project.

"I intend this place to be independent of both politics and the temples, which is why I have disassociated myself from the union in order to build it. I hope now you have a greater understanding of my recent actions and can forgive me for any deceit I may have committed.

"Yours, Devurak."

Onkadal looked scandalised. "He's building a school? A big, fancy *school*? That's why he deserted the lot of us and stole half of my best builders?"

"It's far more than just a fancy school, Onkadal. This will be the ultimate place for education and learning; somewhere that scholars can all come together to work on far bigger research projects than they could manage alone," Hinasi enthused. "Something like Talri-Pekra's Inner Library, except not just for mages. It will completely change how children are taught."

Jindara watched the two of them argue over it. She wasn't that bothered either way herself, but she could see the appeal of it. So long as Devurak wasn't plotting anything detrimental out there, she had no problem with a 'grand place of learning'. The mention of Prince Michael had stirred up some thoughts, however; she had not yet written to him about the warning she had received from the lizard Xhih'a, and she scribbled a note to remind herself. She also wondered how regularly he had been contacting her siblings, and what they talked about. Tironde had said in her last letter that he had inspired her to leave in search of Trizes, Hinasi had mentioned getting letters from him, and now Devurak had got this university idea from him. What exactly was the foreign Prince playing at?

~~~~~~~~~~~~~~~~~~~~~~~~~

Enkarini looked around the clearing warily. The devil had led the way to a clearing large enough for Maldor to land comfortably, and now stood watching her, his grey eyes like chips of flint in the weak sunlight that made it this far down. She expected something to happen; some kind of ambush, or an attack, but the clearing was almost silent. "So, what do you want?" she asked him. He obviously had some reason for bringing them here, and the sooner she found out what it was, the sooner they could get away and start looking for a weak spot in the shield.

"You." He smiled, the expression twisting his features oddly. "I've been able to sense you since your mother fell pregnant with you; the amount of power you have is remarkable. So much potential, and you have only scratched the surface so far."

She drew back slightly. "That woman said something about sharing the line, and a temple; I'm not interested in that, so if that's what you're after you'll have to find someone else," she said.

"Oh, not in the slightest," he replied. "I have my own ways of gathering followers. I simply need someone with a lot of power to help me break this confinement. The shield over this place was created three hundred years ago, by my sister and her worshippers, the Church of the Mistress. They imprisoned me here for freeing the souls they were using to enhance their dark magic."

She frowned, trying to process this new information. She had always assumed that he was the wicked one, as he had trapped her sister here and chased her through the Forest, but it seemed like Kandrina had possibly just been trapped by this shield, and the red woman was actually behind it all.

He continued. "I have no ill intentions towards you, or your family, unlike the Mistress. I simply ask that you assist me in breaking this spell so that I can escape. With your abilities, and some help from your dragon friend there, you should be able to find a way to bring this shield down."

"Listen, I just want to find my sister and take her home safely," Enkarini said. "I don't care what's going on here, I don't want anything to do with raising a temple. If you can help us get out of here and find Kandrina, then I'll come back and help you get out afterwards." She looked him right in the eye; she had watched her father and Wordarla negotiate with awkward and stubborn customers often enough and had cribbed this firm technique straight from the dwarven woman when she spoke to her suppliers. She wanted Kandrina safe more than anything, and this shield spell would probably be easier to break from the outside than from in here.

He stared at her a moment before nodding. "Follow that path. At the end you will find a place that was once called Haven. It marks the centre of the Forest, and the place where the shield is at its weakest. I cannot breach it, but the two of you should be able to break through, if you concentrate your magic enough." He pointed down a narrow path, that Enkarini was certain had not been there before. "I will keep the Mistress away from you long enough for you to get there. Find your sister and remember our deal."

With that, he melted into the trees, leaving them alone. Enkarini stared at the place where he had vanished, wondering what she had just agreed to. Still, if he couldn't get out, there was no way he'd be able to come after her. "Let's go," she said to Maldor. The dragon slowly turned and made his way down the narrow path. "Should I have done that? Made a deal with him?" she asked after several minutes of silence.

"Ideally, I would suggest not, young one. However, circumstances are less than ideal, and thine actions were necessary," he said. "Had thou refused his offer, he would likely have become angered and attempted to trap us here. We can now escape this place unhindered. Thou may find a way out of thy deal in the future."

She wasn't quite reassured by that, but at least what Maldor had just said agreed with her own line of thought. She could always worry about her deal with the devil after Kandrina was home and safe. Maybe she could even help find a way around it or explain why Enkarini either should or shouldn't keep her promise.

After a while, they started seeing stones and collapsed walls. The trees slowly thinned, and they came to a ruined hamlet, the only indication it had ever existed being the foundations of a dozen houses and the remains of a well. She slid off Maldor's back and walked over to a large, rounded stone that stood by itself. There were letters carved into it, in a script she was unfamiliar with, but the multitude of translation spells she and Soris had cast allowed her to read it: Welcome to Haven.

"The shield is weak here. It would take far too much time to decipher and break down from this side, but I believe we can use brute force to get through it," Maldor said softly.

"Do you think people lived here?" she asked. "What happened, why did they leave?"

Maldor looked around at the ruins. "I know not, young one, but there is an ill aspect in the air. We ought not linger too long." The distant sound of some disturbance reached them. "Come. Let us examine this spell to discover its weakness," he said to her.

Enkarini left the stone sign and went back to the dragon's side. She didn't quite know what he meant by 'examine' the spell, but she trusted that he knew what he was doing. They stood for a moment, staring up at the small bit of sky visible to them. If she squinted, she could just make out a sort of shiny patch, far above them. She tried to point it out to Maldor, but he said he couldn't see it.

She closed her eyes, letting her thoughts wander. Sometimes she found that just leaving her mind to its own devices gave her better ideas than if she actually tried to think about things. The shiny bit she could see was probably a weak spot in the shield spell, but how could they disrupt it enough to get through? For some reason, something Remlika had said to her over a year ago leapt to the forefront of her thoughts. When she had first started learning about magic, both of the twins had mentioned the Colourless, and how magic would interfere with their electrical energy. Remlika had wondered aloud if it worked in reverse, if electricity could disrupt magical energy.

She opened her eyes, this new idea begging to be tried. She focused her sight on the shiny patch of sky, took careful aim, and sent a bolt of conjured lightning towards it. The second it made contact; a small, burnt-looking gap appeared briefly before resealing itself. "Electricity will break it, at least for a moment while we get through," she exclaimed happily.

"Well done, young one. Thou art truly gifted," Maldor said, clearly impressed. She climbed onto his back again, and he took off, hovering just above the treetops. "Cast the most powerful thunderbolt in thy capability, I shall lend thee some of my magic to enhance it," he instructed her.

Enkarini took a moment to gather herself and cast the biggest lightning spell she had learnt. As she released the magic, she felt a sort of charge flowing through her, and the bolt of electricity that shot from her fingers came out so strongly that it almost knocked her off the dragon's back. It exploded against the shield above them and burnt a hole large enough for Maldor to fly through. He flew straight upwards, turned in the air, and took off.

She looked back, and saw the shield starting to repair itself again. Before it was out of sight, the hole had shrunk by half, and a web of silvery lines criss-crossed the gap that remained. "How much longer until we reach the desert?"

"I would guess we will arrive by sunrise tomorrow, if there are no more delays," Maldor replied. "We have lost some hours here; should I ascend to escape the influence of the shield and fly faster? It will mean thou shalt have to endure some cold and damp."

"If you can do it, go ahead," Enkarini said without hesitation. She could put up with a little discomfort if it meant getting away from this creepy place and finding Kandrina quicker.

~~~~~~~~~~~~~~~~~~~~~~~~~~~~~

Braklarn stumbled down the narrow steps, wary of making his light any brighter in case there was someone unfriendly waiting down here. After almost two weeks of observation, during which not a single person came to use the hidden entrance, he had realised that it was not being used anymore. Perhaps his clumsy attempt at entry had warned them of its discovery.

Free to examine it fully, he had thoroughly checked the concealment and locking spells that surrounded it and found an identifying spell, one that only allowed certain people through. He had eventually fooled it into giving him access and had crawled through into the rooms beyond. The few rooms he had looked into so far had been nothing more than storerooms, full of dust and cobwebs. A narrow, rickety set of stairs led down into the basement, so he had conjured a small light and headed down. He finally reached the bottom and squinted around. The place seemed empty, so he brightened his light to get a proper look.

The room he found himself in was a smaller, darker version of the main temple hall upstairs; instead of white marble adorned with flowers and lanterns, the altar was dark granite with a single unlit candle on it. There were no pews or seats of any kind, but a handful of threadbare mats scattered on the floor. The clockwise spiral had been drawn on the wall behind the altar; at first Braklarn thought it was dark brownish-red paint, but a closer look told him otherwise. He shuddered and moved towards a small wooden doorway to the side of the altar.

It creaked open at his touch, revealing a long corridor with heavy iron doors at regular intervals. Proceeding with caution, he peered into the rooms through small windows in the doors; they contained nothing but mouldy straw in the corners. He walked quicker, a cold, tight feeling in his chest and the urge to flee rising. A door at the end of the corridor came into view, made of carved wood rather than iron, and he hoped it was unlocked.

The handle would not turn, but with

his nerves starting to get the better of him, he decided to just break it down, check out the room beyond and then get out. A simple fire spell melted both handle and lock, and scorched the wood surrounding it. The door then swung open silently, revealing a small room with a cluttered set of shelves at the back. He made his conjured light as bright as he could, and quickly sifted through the contents of the shelves. Most of it was old junk; broken bottles, scrap parchment, empty inkwells and the like. There were two dusty books that looked as though they could be useful, and a scroll that bore the seal of the High Priest. Braklarn seized them and headed back out of the temple as quickly as he could.

Once he was back in his own study, he immediately lit a fire in the hearth and stoked it until it was roaring. Despite it being a very warm early summer night, he felt a chill down his spine that would not leave him. He pulled his chair as close to the flames as he could without sitting in them and started to read the two books. One had no title and seemed to be a poorly translated dwarven account of the myths and legends surrounding the three spiral gods. The only thing in there Braklarn had not already found out was a claim that the Mistress had once been worshipped as a fire goddess, alongside her brother the forest god.

The other book was titled 'Chaos' and proved to be far more informative; it gave details of several rituals involved in the worship of the chaos god and described a 'waking ritual' near the back. Parts of this had been underlined, with a note in the margin saying 'Did not work. Rethink.' He set the book aside to study in depth later and picked up the scroll. The seal looked fresh, but the scroll itself was old and tattered, bearing a faded, intricate ink mark over both ends. The ink mark was a relic from before wax seals became common; if the scroll had been opened or tampered with, the pattern would no longer line up properly, and the recipient would know the contents were not secure. Of course, a patient letter thief could realign the marks, so more people started using wax and the ink marks fell out of use. They did, however, tell Braklarn that this scroll was much older than he had imagined it would be.

He broke the seal and read: 'To my

successor. If you are reading this, you must be one of the few left of our hidden faith. It has been almost a century since our Lord was banished from the mortal realm, yet his followers and his greatness live on through us. Perhaps it is longer for you; I write this letter from the past, in the hope that the temple of Chaos will survive the purge. I leave our holy texts hidden in this storeroom alongside our ritual items. May fair fortune smile upon your efforts, and the god reward you when he awakes.' There was a scrawl beneath that Braklarn assumed was a signature, followed by another note in different handwriting.

'My successor – this note has been written in great haste. I suspect it will not prove necessary, as we are close to waking our Lord of Chaos. He has been absent for almost two hundred years now, but I believe we have found a way. Unfortunately, our small place in Tewen may have been discovered, so we have moved back to the original temple in Manak. If you read this, know that there are friends of Chaos within the Creator's temple. You will know them by the sign of the spiral on their wrist. Yours in brotherhood, Gistran.'

Braklarn put down the scroll. Finally, he had some solid proof that something rotten was at the core of the temple, and Gistran was definitely involved. This explained why the false acolytes were aligned with the Creator's temple, and nowhere else; Gistran had clearly scouted out those who worshipped Chaos and brought them in under a guise of piety. He pulled the books over again and flicked through, searching for the rest of the pieces. He could not find anything that explicitly asked for human sacrifices, but several involved creating uncertainty, fear and doubt among the People. Having a crazed murderer on the loose had certainly achieved that.

He snapped the book shut and hid it in a drawer of his desk along with the scroll and the rest of his notes. If the worshippers of Chaos had taken their cult to Manak, he would have to follow them there to conclude his investigation. Regardless of what god they claimed to kneel to, there was still at least one killer among them, and he intended to bring that killer to justice. There was also the matter of Dekarem, Kolena, and anyone else they had enchanted into doing their bidding. He would break the news to Jindara tonight and transport out there in the morning.

~~~~~~~~~~~~~~~~~~~~~~~~~~~~~

Enkarini squinted down at the expanse of yellowish sand beneath her. The sunlight was harsh, with little shade or relief. She didn't know what kind of supplies Kandrina and Remlik had with them, but she doubted they could last much longer in these conditions. Kandrina was not answering her when she tried to speak to her using mind contact, and she didn't know why. Maldor had suggested it could be that Kandrina had fallen unconscious, or perhaps had closed her mind for some reason. Either way, Enkarini wanted to find her quickly.

They had been flying over the desert for an hour, keeping the edge of the Forest on their right, when she spotted three people trailing slowly across the endless sand. "There, they're there!" she called to Maldor, who wheeled about and started to descend. He landed a short distance from the three figures, who all turned to see what was casting the huge shadow that had fallen across them. Enkarini slid from his back and gaped at her sister.

Kandrina had grown painfully thin, her cheekbones sticking out and her eyes appearing larger than usual; she had stripped most of her clothes off because of the heat, and a painful redness covered her skin. Remlik looked much the same, except without the severe sunburn. The odd creature that accompanied them had backed away in panic when it saw the dragon descending, but now it edged closer, eyeing her warily.

Enkarini stepped forwards, her concern for her sister overriding everything else at that moment. "Kandrina, come on. Let's get home," she said, holding out a hand. "You too, Remlik. Your sister's worried about you."

"Now I know I'm losing it. This can't be happening, this damn heat is making me see things," Kandrina muttered. "You're not here. You're at home in Tewen and there isn't a massive great dragon sitting there." She screwed her eyes shut and held her head tightly.

Remlik stared, his eyes unfocused. "Well, at least we're going mad together,

Kandi. I can see them too."

"I am here, Kandrina, I came to take you home," Enkarini said pleadingly. "I can explain it all, but you need to come with me now, you really don't look well." She wished she had brought some water with her, both of them looked very ill. The creature was looking at her curiously, its head tipped to one side, as though it was unsure what to make of her and Maldor. She looked back at it, wondering if it could understand her.

"Perhaps thy sister and her friend will find our presence more believable after a glass of water and something to eat," Maldor suggested.

Enkarini turned, about to say that they didn't have any water or food with them and saw that he had magicked up a large pitcher of iced water and a plate of savoury biscuits. "Good idea," she said with a smile. She poured a glass out and offered it to Kandrina. "Here, you need to drink something. You must be thirsty after being out here so long."

"Right. My little sister has arrived on a black dragon to give me a glass of water in the desert. I'd accept, but I can't drink a hallucination," Kandrina replied.

"You always were a stubborn little madam," Enkarini retorted, quoting something their father had said some years ago. She flung the contents of the glass over Kandrina, thinking it might at least make her realise the water was real.

Kandrina spluttered for a moment, staring at her sister. Suddenly, she threw herself on Enkarini with a yell of joy, hugging the younger girl tightly. "You really are here! How did you... You're going to have to explain this," she said.

Enkarini grinned back at her sister. Now they had found each other again, she could stop worrying; they would get home, and Kandrina would be fine. "Definitely, but first let's get going. I don't think we should stick around in this desert for too long," she said, gesturing towards Maldor. "Can you fly us back to Tewen?"

"That may not be advisable, young one. Thy people may panic should they see me over their town. I shall fly thee back to the plains where thou first summoned me," he said as they all climbed onto his back.

"That's fine, I can take them home from there. Thank you, Maldor." She turned to face the other three. "You'll need to hold on tight while he takes off, it's quite a leap into the air," she told them.

In answer, Kandrina and Remlik gripped the hard, ridged scales in front of them. Remlik made some noise to the creature, who had climbed up behind him, and it put its arms around his waist. Maldor leapt skywards once more and began flying back towards the Forest.

Chapter Six:
Back to Study

Enkarini smiled to herself as she wandered around the bookshelves. She had been smiling almost constantly for the last two days, since arriving home with her sister. At Remlik's suggestion, Maldor had diverted around the north of the Forest and over some swamps to avoid getting caught in the shield again. The journey had taken almost a week, but at least they had not been caught by the red woman or the devil – who were actually called the Mistress and the Tall One, according to Kandrina.

She'd said something about them being old gods, and that the Mistress wanted to revive her temple using the bloodline of the last high priestess, who was apparently some long-distant ancestor of theirs. The two of them had not been able to get together for a proper catch up yet, but Enkarini didn't much like what she'd heard about this Mistress so far. Perhaps she had done right by agreeing to help the Tall One get out of her trap...

"Psst."

The whisper distracted her, and she looked around for its source. "What?" she whispered back, spotting Soris hiding between two shelves.

He beckoned her over urgently. "I did it; I finally managed to get a copy of the Archive key. There was an enchantment on it to prevent anyone copying it, but I got around that," he murmured. There was a faintly smug look on his face. "Guess how, go on."

"I don't know, cancelled out the anti-copying spell?"

Soris smirked. "Nope. I couldn't have replaced it afterwards, so she'd have known someone had taken it. I wondered though, what if someone just made a mould of it or something, then made another key using that? So, I took it to a key maker in Entamar and asked him to make a copy for me. It seems the spell only protected it against magical copying," he said, the smug grin definitely showing now. "Then I just returned the original and copied the copy. Glissia doesn't even know it was gone."

Enkarini smiled; it really was brilliant how Soris managed to think up things like that. "That's fantastic."

"I know," he said smugly, before becoming suddenly serious. "She asked where you were, though. Everyone did. I kept them going in circles for a couple of days; told your dad you were at Caiara's and everyone else you had stayed home unwell. It fell apart when your dad went over to speak to Aila though. Of course, she said you weren't there, and he came rushing into the temple in a panic. I had to come clean about the spell, and where you'd gone. I suppose your dad's already spoken to you about it all," he said.

She nodded. "He wasn't sure whether to be cross with me for being so reckless, or glad I'd found Kandrina and got her home safely. So, I'm being punished by not being allowed to practice alchemy at home for a month and rewarded with a fancy gold cauldron once my ban is lifted," she smiled. "Was anyone else cross when they found out?"

"I think Glissia wants to ask you a few questions, but nobody's really mad about it, since you were saving your sister and all. Well, Aila's pretty livid, but she's angry with Caiara, not you."

Enkarini was confused. "Wait, why is Cai's mum angry with her? She didn't do anything wrong, did she?"

"Some absurd superstitious rubbish. Apparently, she doesn't want her precious daughter to ruin her chances of joining the temple by associating with a dark sorceress," Soris told her. "Caiara's in a right state. Her mum kept her at home for a week, she was only allowed to come back here yesterday."

"Is she here?" Enkarini asked, concerned for her friend.

Soris nodded. "She's hiding in the Archive. I gave her a copy of the key, too, since she's supposed to help out with our investigation." He handed her a heavy, ornate key. "Here's yours."

She thanked him quickly and rushed up to the balcony. Luckily there were not many people in the Library on Eighth Days, and the entrance hall was deserted. She slipped through the Archive door and closed it behind her. It seemed eerie, being there alone. The place was almost silent, except for the faint sound of pages turning. She followed the sound, dust muffling her footsteps, and found a slim, bald girl sitting at a table facing the wall. "Hello?" she called, unsure of who this girl was.

The girl jumped and turned around, and Enkarini recognised her friend. "Cai? What happened?" The last time Enkarini had seen her, Caiara had a sheet of reddish blonde hair that fell nearly to her hips.

Caiara turned away, her dark blue eyes sparkling with tears. "Mum says I'm not supposed to talk to you, because she thinks you'll teach me black magic and lead me astray. She cut off my hair as a punishment, because I lied to her about spending time with you."

"Why has she suddenly got a problem with me?" Enkarini burst out. "Last month she was fine with you coming over for the night, now she thinks I'm some evil witch?"

Caiara sniffed. "I don't know why, but she always has, ever since you showed me your shadow cloud at the Festival. I told her

I was staying at the temple the night I came over to yours," she said in a very small voice. "I know you're not what she says, and I've tried to tell her, but she won't listen. I don't want to fall out with you over this." She was almost pleading now.

Enkarini went to kneel by the chair. "We won't fall out. It's not your fault what your mother thinks," she reassured Caiara. "She can't treat you like this, though. Really, it's her own fault that you had to lie, since if she wasn't being so horrid about things you would have felt you could be honest." She thought for a moment. "Can't you get out of there? You're nearly of age anyway, she can't keep you at home forever. Maybe you could stay with a friend for a couple of months?"

Caiara rubbed her nose with her sleeve. "I already thought of that. I tried running away four years ago, but I don't know anything about hiding, and she knows where all my friends live. She'd probably just come and drag me back there," she said glumly.

"Not if you come to mine," Enkarini replied. "We live in Tewen, so she couldn't get there easily, and since I'm such a scary, wicked witch she won't want to come anywhere near my lair." She couldn't help grinning as she said it; the idea that anyone could think she was that evil was ridiculous.

"Won't your dad mind?" the older girl asked as she dried her eyes.

"I don't think so. It wouldn't be forever, anyway, just until you can get yourself sorted. Besides, I think he misses having Kandrina around the house, and now she's living with Remlik he'd probably be glad to have someone else around." She remembered they had missed her sister's coming of age, as they had still been with the dwarves, so she thought it might be nice to celebrate Caiara's. "Come home with me tonight, and we can talk to him about it."

Caiara smiled tentatively. "Alright then. Oh, while we're in here, I wanted to show you something," she said, some of her usual chattiness returning. She pulled a book closer and opened it to a marker. "I've been looking through these old things for some clues about the locked room, and I found this. It looks like a diary or something, but I can't read it. Since you did all those translation spells, I thought you might be able to."

Enkarini squinted at the old, curly writing. She admired the artful way the writer had made the letters, but why couldn't these old books be a little plainer, so people could actually read them? She let her eyes fuzz over a bit so the translation magic could work easier, and bits of meaning started coming through. "Well, I can't read a lot of it yet, but there's something about a gateway, and I think it's talking about two spells, one for opening and one for closing," she said slowly. "I'll take it home, and we can work with it tonight. You think it might be about the room?"

"I think so. It was well hidden at the back of a shelf, behind a load of other books, so I guess someone didn't want it to be found or read. Since the only thing around here that anyone's that secretive about is the locked room, it made sense," Caiara told her.

She had to agree. Everything else in the Library was freely available for study; they weren't even told what they could and couldn't read in the Archive, it was only locked so that the fragile old books weren't damaged by constant unsupervised use. "Let's go and tell Soris, then we can head home and talk to Father. I'm sure he'll be fine with you staying with us for a few months," she said excitedly, leaping up from the floor. They both skipped out of the room, careful to lock the door behind them once they left.

~~~~~~~~~~~~~~~~~~~~~~~~~~

Jindara ran her finger around the edge of her glass, so deep in thought that she barely heard the whining noise it made. The people of Tewen were content with the reforms she was making and had decided in favour of the union becoming a looser alliance of the tribes. Things were going well in that regard, but the former people of Manak were becoming restless and angry.

They had, or so the more vocal among them were saying, been sidelined and ignored ever since the Lizard War. They were homeless, living off the mercy and good graces of others, and nothing had been done to find them new homes. Nothing had been offered to help them recover from the losses they had suffered. With the breakdown of the union, they were now without a leader. Some had settled into other towns and considered themselves members of their adopted tribe. Others refused to let go of their Manak heritage and were insisting that they needed a new town to make their own.

As far as Jindara knew, nobody had problems with those who had adopted a new tribe. She didn't even see a problem with those who wanted to remain Manak and would gladly offer them help to build a new town for themselves, but only after she had dealt with the reforms in Tewen. Apart from that, she had the issue of Xhih'a's warning to deal with. She had written to Prince Michael about it, asking for his advice, and he had replied only a week later. She snatched the folded paper from her table and reread it, hoping for some titbit of information she had not found the first dozen times.

'Dear Jindara, I regret that I cannot offer insight as to why the green dragons may be enraged enough to come after your People; their current temperament is one mystery we have yet to solve. We may be

181

able to help with the defence of your lands, and I have enclosed several military strategies for protecting your People. Unfortunately, our own air forces are occupied with an issue here, or I would have a couple of squadrons sent down to you.

'Your sister has arrived safely and has asked that I enclose a personal letter with this. The mages she brought with her are settling in well, and currently working on potential solutions to our troubles, but I will not bore you with the details of all our woes. Tironde suggested that we ask the dragons here in Trizes whether they could be of any assistance to you, and we have sent out an emissary. I will inform you when we have a reply. Until then, I hope the papers I have sent are of some use. Yours, Prince Michael.'

She had given the tactical papers to her generals, who had immediately begun drilling the soldiers in methods of defence against attacks from above. Some of Tewen's more skilled mages had started working on a protective spell that would cover the town, to at least provide some measure of shielding. Jindara had also passed on the information to the other tribes and begun thinking of ways to either evacuate the town or shelter the townspeople from the attacks. She was considering the possibility of building underground shelters, as described in one of Prince Michael's papers, but to build one large enough to hold the entire population of Tewen would be a massive undertaking.

Evacuating the whole town wasn't practical, as there would be nowhere that could take that many people in for any length of time, and they had no idea when this attack might come. Starting to clear the town when they spotted the dragons approaching wouldn't give them enough time to get everyone out safely. She discarded that idea for the moment and turned her mind back to shields and shelter. Mages could protect the town for a while, but any spell large enough to cover the whole town would have several weaknesses, and eventually fail if the dragons were intent on destruction. Multiple small shields would be stronger, but miss areas, and leave some people unprotected. The underground shelter kept nudging at her, and she wondered if it was necessary to build one large shelter, or if several small shelters would be better...

She bolted upright and seized a piece of parchment. "People could build their own shelters, in their gardens," she said to herself, scribbling it down before she forgot it. "Big enough for their family, small enough to not be a target from the air. It wouldn't save their homes, but at least the people would survive." She drew a rough sketch of the shelter she pictured; a sort of dome shape, sunk into the ground and covered in soil, with a doorway accessible via some steps down. People could sit out any attack in there, maybe keep some food and water supplies in case it went on for a long time. She would have to talk to some of her advisors in the morning, but she was fairly sure this would work.

The only unknown was the type of attacks these dragons might use. She pulled over another bit of parchment and began another letter to Michael:

'Dear Prince Michael, my thanks for your letter and the tactical papers. My generals have found them most useful so far. I am glad Tironde has arrived safely, and I hope you are taking good care of her. I enclose a personal letter for her, if you would be kind enough to pass it on.

'I have some questions about the green dragons, so that we can get a better idea of what we might have to face. What sort of powers or abilities do they have? I recall you mentioning that they were guardians of nature, do they perhaps have some control over plant or animal life? Are they likely to attack physically, and if so, how strong are they? Do they have any particular weaknesses? Any information you can provide would be useful, as our own books on dragons are more myth than fact.

'There has been a change in politics here, perhaps Tironde has mentioned; our tribes are no longer united, but some are allied. My siblings Onkadal and Hinasi are now Chiefs of Akram and Bewein respectively, a former general named Garren is Chief of Astator. We are still uncertain of what is happening with the other tribes, but we are hoping to settle things down soon. I hope that your troubles, whatever they are, can be resolved; perhaps there is some way we can be of assistance to you? If there is any way I can help, do let me know. Yours,

Chief Jindara.'

She read over the letter quickly, checking it was all in order before adding her letter for Tironde, sealing it and leaving it on the table for the couriers to pick up. With things as done as she could get them tonight, she drained her glass and sat back in her chair, gazing out of the window. The sky was especially clear and still, giving her a fantastic view of the two moons. She had always loved warm summer nights like this. It was one thing away from perfection...

"If you've finished for the night, perhaps you'd like to bring the rest of that bottle through here," came a seductive purr from the bedroom door. She turned to see Braklarn leaning against the doorframe, wearing nothing but a thin robe. "You look beautiful in the moonlight."

Jindara smiled, picked up the half-full wine bottle, and walked over to him. "Flattery will get you everywhere, my love." She kissed him and led the way into the chamber.

~~~~~~~~~~~~~~~~~~~~

"There you two are. I was starting to think you weren't coming." Soris scowled over at the two girls from his chair in the corner. "What kept you?"

Enkarini shrugged. "We were up late last night. I guess we overslept," she said with a smile. The last few days since Caiara had come to stay with her had been like having one long sleepover. She took the chair beside him, and Caiara sat opposite. "Did you look at the pages I sent you?"

"Yeah. It definitely says gateway, but I can't make out what sort of gateway it means. I think the translation spells might be fading, because there were some parts that just didn't make any sense. It was like trying to read gibberish," he complained. "Maybe we ought to try recasting some of those spells soon."

Caiara frowned at him. "Or maybe it's supposed to be gibberish. Did it occur to you that it might be a code or something? That wouldn't necessarily translate, it would need to be deciphered. If it is someone's diary, and they thought that someone else might read it to find out their secrets, they'd do something to stop that."

"That's a good thought," Enkarini said quickly, as Soris was glaring daggers at the older girl. "So, if it is a code, we'll need to find a way to work it out. Any ideas?"

Soris frowned at the table between them. "There are a few books about codes and encryptions in the library; I think there's one somewhere in the Archive too. It might be worth checking out," he said reluctantly. "Did you manage to get anything else out of the book?"

Enkarini glanced around to check that nobody was nearby before taking it out of her dress pocket. "I'm not sure. A lot of it doesn't make much sense, whether it's code or just the translation spells fading I don't know. It definitely mentions a gateway several times, and there's something about building, or maybe a building, here, and a gathering of travellers," she showed them the page she meant. "Then later it says something about the spell to open the gateway, and close it later." She paused, unsure that what she wanted to say was right. "Somehow, I get the feeling that she wanted it closed when they had come through it. Like it was really important, so nothing could follow them through."

The three were quiet for a moment,

thinking. "That fits in with my theory," Soris mumbled. "I was thinking, maybe this diary belonged to one of the Firsts. If I'm right, it might be about how they got here or where they came from. There aren't many records from back then; in fact, I can only think of one, and it's just a list of names."

"So, if this is a First's diary, maybe the gateway it talks about is the same one they used to come here?" Enkarini looked down at the tattered book in her hands with renewed awe. She was beginning to understand what Kandrina and Remlik had always told her, the sense of wonder and fascination when they discovered something new, the excitement of uncovering things that had been lost for years, even centuries. An idea occurred to her, and she leant forwards to whisper to the other two. "Do you think maybe the gateway still exists? Maybe it's in the locked room?"

Caiara took a breath, ran her hand over the soft stubble on her scalp. "It's possible, but let's not get too ahead of ourselves. We don't even know if this book did belong to a First." She stared pensively into the fireplace for a moment. "Before we go running off with ideas, why don't we try to read a bit more of this diary? Can you remember those translation spells you did?"

"Some of them. We can get hold of the books again though; didn't you say your tutor kept the originals?" Soris asked.

Enkarini nodded. "The originals are in the lizard language, though. If the spells are failing, then we might not be able to read them."

Caiara jumped up. "You got them from the Li Buqu books? Arikele just put them out on the shelves yesterday, I heard her talking about it. I'll go get them," she exclaimed as she ran out of the room.

When she had gone, Soris turned to Enkarini with an exasperated expression. She knew he didn't get along with Caiara, or anybody really, but she wasn't going to ignore her other friends for his sake. "What?" she asked.

"How do you cope with that all the time? She'd drive me mad," he said.

She turned in the chair to face him. "I know she can be a bit, well, energetic sometimes, but she's a nice person. If you give her a chance, she's a really good friend," she told him. "Besides, she needs someone to look out for her right now, and a place to stay. You know what her mother's like. Cai doesn't deserve to be treated that way, nobody does." Aila had come to the temple two weeks ago and hammered on the Library doors, demanding that her daughter go home with her and repent so that she could join the temple. High Priestess Glissia had intervened in the end, and told her that Caiara had chosen to leave home and was staying with a friend, it was her daughter's decision what to do with her life, and if Caiara did not truly want to join the temple then she could not be forced.

Soris looked thoughtful. "Well, I suppose. I'll try to be nice," he said. "She really does annoy me though; nobody's that perky and happy so much of the time."

Enkarini laughed. "Maybe you two should spend more time together, so you make up a whole person. Cai's like the happy half and you're the grumpy half," she teased gently.

"I am not grumpy," he replied, tossing a cushion at her.

Caiara returned with an armful of

books and dropped them on the table. "Is this all of them? I couldn't see any more," she said breathlessly.

"Yes, that's all of them," Enkarini said. "Hey, you know what we could do? We could write the spells down for ourselves, that way if we need them again, we don't have to go looking for these books. People might take them out, and we'd have to wait for them," she suggested.

The other two nodded. "Good idea. Why didn't we think of that last time?" Soris asked. He pulled out some parchment and started looking through the books. "Once we've found them all again, we can go into the practice room and cast them."

Caiara and Enkarini pulled over a book each and flicked through, searching for translation magic. Once they could all read the diary, hopefully it would reveal more secrets about the locked room and the Firsts.

~~~~~~~~~~~~~~~~~~~~~~

Enkarini watched her sister, who looked more like herself now she had eaten a few good meals and treated her sunburn. The two of them had spent the whole afternoon catching up over a tray of biscuits and tea; Enkarini had talked about her studies and how she came to summon the black dragon to come after her sister, and Kandrina about her time in the Forest and what she had discovered or guessed about the two old gods. They had lapsed into silence a few moments ago, and Enkarini was trying to work up the nerve to explain the one thing she had missed out of her tale: her deal with the Tall One.

"So, how did you find this Haven place?" Kandrina asked. "We were wandering around that Forest for weeks, and we never had any clue there was a ruined town in the middle of it."

Enkarini took a deep breath. "Erm, that's the thing. We probably wouldn't have found it, at least not that quickly, but..." She faltered, couldn't meet her sister's pale blue gaze. "Well, we kind of got cornered by the Mistress, and when we got away, he showed up, and said he'd help us escape if we did the same for him. I said I'd work out a way to break down the shield spell after I had found you and brought you home," she said in a rush.

Kandrina stared at her for a few

minutes in disbelief. "You made a bargain with the Tall One?"

"I had no choice, it was the only way I could get out of there," Enkarini tried to explain. "We were already trapped, and when he said he could help us get out I thought it would be best to just agree with him, otherwise he would have tried to stop us leaving. It's not like he can come after me, if he's stuck in there, right? So, I've got time to work out whether I should go back or not," she said.

Kandrina made an odd sound between a sigh and a groan. "He can't come after you physically, but you have no idea what you're dealing with, Enkarini." She raked her fingers through her hair, obviously trying to find the right words for what she had to say. "He can... reach out, into people's minds, he can control them and twist them even from that distance. I suppose some people are more susceptible to it than others. Mother was one of them, he must have done something to her..."

Enkarini was puzzled. "What do you mean? What's Mother got to do with this?"

"I'm not quite sure yet, I'm still trying

to work it out," Kandrina said shakily. "I told you about the connection with the Mistress, how we were descended from the daughter of her last priestess. There's some sort of feud between the Mistress and the Tall One. She wants to rebuild her temple, with someone from the original bloodline as the new priestess. He wants to stop her doing that. This is a theory in progress, but... I think he tried to get Mother on his side, so that she wouldn't help the Mistress. She was carrying you at the time, I remember her acting strange around then. After you were born, she disappeared, and everyone said she had been killed by the Demons, remember?"

"Yes, but what's this got to do with the Tall One?"

"I think he persuaded her to go to the Forest, to join him. I need to look into it deeper, because there's something I'm missing. But if he could affect Mother like that, maybe he can reach you as well." Kandrina cast a worried look at her sister. "I just don't want you to get mixed up in this, it's all too strange and dangerous."

The sisters fell silent again, watching one another in concern. Enkarini knew that

Kandrina was only worried about her; she had often acted as mother instead of big sister when they were younger, and she was still quite protective. Still, Enkarini thought, she was now learning advanced magic and had already proved herself capable of things Kandrina had never dreamt of, so surely she could start making her own choices in life? She didn't want to upset her sister though, so she let go of the thoughts of arguing over it and changed the subject.

"Say, I've actually been meaning to ask you about something for a while, and Remlik too if he's here," she said. "A couple of friends and I are looking into the Firsts; who they were, how they got here, that sort of thing. Do you know much about them?"

"The Firsts?" Kandrina looked surprised, and a little relieved at the change of topic. "What's inspired you to start studying them? I would have thought there'd be more interesting things for you to learn at the Library than some dusty old history."

Enkarini fiddled with her empty cup. "I'm curious. Besides, if what I can do is their Wyld Magic, it makes sense to find out about them and what they knew."

Kandrina poured out fresh tea for them both. "I can't say I recall a lot of what I learnt about them, not that I knew much to forget. Remlik," she called up the stairs. "Enkarini has a question for you." They heard a distant reply, and footsteps overhead. "I'm sure Remlik will help if he can. I don't think there are many records about the Firsts though."

Remlik came into view, covered in cobwebs. "I'll be having serious words with my sister tonight. I can't believe she let the place get this filthy," he grumbled as he brushed off the worst of it and sat down. "Anyway, what can I help you with, Enkarini?"

"I'm trying to find out about the Firsts, my friends and I want to know more about them and their magic," she explained briefly.

"That's a very obscure project; as I'm sure Kandi mentioned, not many documents have survived from their time, and a lot has been lost or destroyed over the centuries. If I remember the basics I learnt, they were a band of mages who came to these lands about three thousand years ago through some sort of magical gate, then separated into like-minded groups which became the tribes. I have a book upstairs that tells the story, but there aren't many details in it," he said. "As far as I know, most of the in-depth texts that mention the Firsts are kept at Talri-Pekra's main library in Bewein, so you're probably at the best place to be researching this already. Remlika could know a little more, since there's such a connection between magic and the Firsts she might have come across them in one of her spell books," he suggested.

Enkarini nodded. "I'll ask her when I see her tomorrow; she said she wanted to come and see how I'm getting on with my studies." She finished her drink and stood. "I ought to head back now, I promised Father I'd be home for dinner."

Kandrina grimaced. "That reminds me, I haven't been to see Father since we got home. I'll walk you back; there's something I need to tell him anyway. Don't wait up, Remlik, this is going to take a while," she said, casting him a sideways look. Remlik's only response was to raise his cup and grin.

Chapter Seven:
The Diary's Secrets

Soris and Caiara glared at each other over the table. They had all been poring over the diary for hours, slowly deciphering one word at a time. The two of them had bickered over every single one, and Enkarini had been forced to yell at them so they would concentrate on the diary, not their disagreements. For a moment, she watched the pair try to stare each other down, then shook her head and returned to work.

Caiara had found an old book in the Archive that described a code similar to the one used in the diary, so they had been using it as a guide for their own attempts to read the diary. It was still hard work, as there were some differences between the coding methods, but between the decoder and the Li Buqu translation spells they had managed to at least roughly decipher most of the diary.

The book had belonged to Astrid Torver, the youngest of the Firsts, apparently only twenty-three at the time of writing. She had decided to chronicle the events before and after the Exodus, as she called it – the mages leaving Trizes and coming to Slokos. She had encoded her writing in case the book fell into the hands of any non-mage that might seek to misuse the information. There was a lot of history within the text, some of which had been interesting, but most had not. Soris had lingered over several of those passages, but Enkarini had found a lot of it quite dull and skipped over them quickly.

It also contained details of the gateway the mages had used to escape Trizes, and these were the pages they were working to interpret exactly right. A mistranslated diary entry would at worst only cause some confusion. A mistranslated spell could potentially cause disaster, so each of the three was performing separate translations, which they then exchanged and compared. They did not take any version as correct until they had all independently reached the same conclusion, but things would have gone a lot quicker if Caiara and Soris had not stubbornly contradicted each other at every stage.

Enkarini sighed, pushed the decoder book away and once again read over the translation they had so far:

'This gateway is like nothing seen before. The others and I combined our magic, along with that of some of our Dragon friends and mentors, to infuse the great device with enough power to cross vast distances in mere seconds. Bennett and Theresa call it a hole in space, a shortcut from one side of this world to another. I cannot pretend to understand the concepts they speak of; I am in awe of the power contained within the device, and glad of Paul's bravery in being the first to venture through.

'He reports that the land there is green and lush, not unlike the Dragons' valley in which we have taken refuge. After his return, the gateway was closed to prevent wild creatures stumbling through, but we shall reopen it soon to make our final exit from these lands where we are unwelcome. Once we arrive in our new home, the device will be sealed and deactivated, so that our persecutors cannot pursue us.'

In the original diary, this entry had

been followed by a drawing of the device mentioned. It looked like an arrangement of five upright columns and a small sphere in the centre, all connected by fine strands of something. Astrid had drawn faint rays of light emitting from the sphere. Two short entries came next:

'One of us must remain behind to close this side of the gateway. There is no way to choose, so we shall all draw lots tonight. Tomorrow we step through the gate and depart these lands forever.' Then: 'Luke Miller will stay to seal the gate here. Theresa wept when he drew the short straw; I think they are fond of each other. She said she would remain with him, but he insists that she leaves with us. Perhaps there will be a way for him to follow us later.'

The last entry that concerned the gateway was only half interpreted:

'The gateway is sealed. We have all escaped to a land of our own; all except noble Luke. A handful of our band of mages chose to stay with him, to begin a settlement among the Dragons, and I wish them all the best. Perhaps our descendants will rediscover one another many years from now.

'The others are making plans to spread out, discover more of this new land and find places to call their homes. I may head towards the coast; Paul tells me there is a fine expanse of golden beach far to the east of here. Theresa intends to remain in this place, near the gateway, in case some contact can be established with those left behind, or Luke and his fellows find a way to join us. She has asked that I write instructions for the future, so that generations to come may know how to return to our ancestral lands if they so wish. I do not know why they would wish to, but I shall do as Theresa asks.

'The power held within the great device can be accessed only by a blood relative of those who gave their magic to it; that is, Theresa, Bennett, Paul, Mark, Rachel, Alec, William, Enyeto or myself. He or she must step into the device, take hold of the connecting filaments, and allow the...'

Enkarini laid the translation aside and rubbed her eyes. "If you two are done being argumentative, I think I've got the next part worked out," she said.

"The rest of the instructions? Same here. Shall we exchange and compare then?" Soris replied, handing his page of notes across to her. Enkarini passed hers to Caiara, who gave hers to Soris, and the three of them read:

'... allow the contained magic to flow through and mingle with his/her own. Then he/she must place a hand upon the sphere, incanting five times the words *allow us safe passage through the void*. He/she must keep contact with the sphere throughout the reaction; it will grow hot, emit sparks of lightning and vibrate fiercely, but this will not harm the caster of the spell if it is done properly. When the spell is complete, the sphere will become ice cold. The moment it does this, the caster must release it and step outside of the device immediately, to allow the gate to open fully in empty space. It will appear as a silvery-grey egg, floating above the sphere.

'Theresa tells me she will build a grand library around the gateway, and the device will be secured in a quiet room with the ancient spell *asi-waju* to ensure that nobody can interfere with it.'

Caiara was the first to finish. "Well Rini, yours is the same as mine bar two grammatical slips. Soris?"

He looked up from Caiara's notes. "This looks much the same as mine. I think we've cracked it," he said, smiling at Caiara for the first time.

"I think you're right. Yours matches up with mine," Enkarini told them as she finished reading. She put Soris' scratchy notes down and took a moment to rest her head on the table while Caiara carefully copied the last sections onto their master copy. This was Caiara's job because she had the neatest handwriting of the three.

Soris pushed his chair back and stretched. "That took forever. So, are we going to try out this spell? See if we can at least get into the room?"

Enkarini looked up at him. "Now? It's getting a bit late, Soris. Maybe we should go home, get some sleep and try it tomorrow," she suggested.

"Actually, it might be worth a look now," Caiara said. "Tomorrow there will probably be too many people around; right now, there's nobody here but us and

Arikele, and she's still busy tidying the library after Nerania knocked that shelf over this afternoon."

Enkarini thought it over and nodded. They gathered up their notes, left the Archive and checked the entrance hall was clear before moving across the balcony to the locked door. Caiara rubbed her hands together in anticipation. "Here we go," she said, stepping forwards. "*Asi-waju!*" There was a flash of yellow light, but the door remained stubbornly locked.

"You probably didn't say it right," Soris told her. "Let me try." He nudged her aside and attempted the spell himself, with the same results.

Enkarini had been checking the translation while the others cast at the door. She wondered if the spell to open the door also needed a direct blood relation of a First to work it properly, like the gateway device did. She pointed this out to the other two.

"Maybe, but aren't we all distant descendants of the Firsts? There were only a few hundred mages that came through, so their children and grandchildren and whatever must have all intermarried somewhere along the line," Caiara said.

Soris frowned slightly, looking first at the door, then at Enkarini. "Or maybe it needs someone who can do the same kind of magic as the Firsts. We know magic has changed through the centuries, but you're able to do the old magic somehow. See if you can unlock it," he murmured, stepping aside for her.

She moved forwards, feeling slightly apprehensive, and took a moment to calm herself before whispering the spell. The flash of light hit the door, as it had for the other two, but this time it swung open. The three looked at each other in glee and had just taken a step towards it when they heard a voice behind them.

"I see your curiosity is not easily satisfied," she said. They whirled around to see the High Priestess watching them from the top of the stairs, her expression unreadable. "Come with me." They sheepishly followed her down the stairs, each hoping they were not in too much trouble.

~~~~~~~~~~~~~~~~~~~~~~~~~~

Braklarn wandered through the ruins,

occasionally poking at a bit of crumbled stone or charred wood. How the former residents of this place could expect to recover any of it was beyond him. Officially, Jindara had sent him out to survey what was left of Manak and report back how much of it could be salvaged or rebuilt. She was trying to appease the handful of agitators who were stirring trouble among the Manak people, and he could not blame her; she had enough to worry about right now without tribal discontent flaring up again.

They had both agreed not to say anything about the real reason for his trip to the old town, as news of the Creator's high priest being involved in a plot to wake the Chaos god would cause a lot of panic. He hoped to find the killer and deal with Gistran relatively quietly, so that as few people as possible became aware of – and potentially involved in – this dangerous cult.

He had combed through his books for any mention of Manak's Chaos temple and found a reference in an obscure text about the Creator, and how he 'reformed from his fragmented self' when the tribes united. It had said his most glorious temple had been built on the site of another, once devoted to an absent god of the Manak. The book had not specified which god it meant, but Braklarn was willing to bet it referred to Chaos, Manak's only absent god that he knew of. So, he was hunting through the rubble for the wreckage of the old temple, but it was not easy. With no landmarks or even streets to guide him, he had quickly lost his bearings.

A gleam of silver caught his eye in the late afternoon sunlight, and he turned towards it, hoping for the remains of the silver spire that had once topped the temple's bell tower. Instead, he saw an abandoned necklace hanging from a beam, swaying slightly in the summer breeze. He almost turned away in disappointment, before he noticed movement in the wrecked house.

"Who's there?" he called softly. A faint whimper answered him, and he edged closer. "If you're hurt, I can help you, but you need to come out first."

Slowly, a ragged, trembling form emerged from the ruins. Braklarn took a step back, fully aware this could be a trap. The man crawled out into the open and, seemingly exhausted by the effort, collapsed on the cracked cobbles of the street. He lay there mumbling to himself, and Braklarn was unsure if the man even knew he was there. He approached carefully and crouched a few feet from him.

The mumbled words were a little clearer now, and he could make out things like 'ritual' and 'escape' several times. Suddenly, the man gasped and bolted upright, making Braklarn leap backwards and shield himself. The man looked straight at him, and he finally recognised his old friend Dekarem, though the fuzzy ginger hair that had sprouted all over his scalp and chin looked most unnatural on the usually shorn and shaven mage.

"Braklarn! Thank all the gods, I'd almost given up! We have to get out of here, and you have to help me get rid of this damned spell, it's driving me crazy," he whispered so fast that the words blurred together.

"What spell? What's going on out here?"

Dekarem shook his head frantically. "Not here, not now, they've been looking for me and I could go back under any minute. Get us back to Tewen, we'll be safe there and I can explain some of this." Braklarn took his friend's arm and transported them both back to his study in Tewen. The Chaos cult would have to wait a while longer.

~~~~~~~~~~~~~~~~~~~~~~~

The three of them fidgeted anxiously, uncertain of what to expect from the High Priestess; were they about to be scolded, disciplined, thrown out of the Library? Soris' gaze flitted about, his hands clenched and twisted together in front of him, he couldn't have looked more guilty if he tried. Did she know about the Archive key copies?

Glissia locked the door and walked around the nervous trio to sit at her desk. Enkarini caught her eye and was surprised to see no anger in her expression. In fact, she almost looked pleased. "So, I understand the three of you have been working together on this project for a while now; would you let me in on the secret?"

Enkarini started to explain. "Well, it

sort of started because I was curious about the locked room on the balcony..." Over the next hour the story unfolded, including their illicit Archive visits, the experimental magic from the Li Buqu books and their translation of some of the Firsts' books. Glissia had simply listened, which they were all glad of in a way, as they could just explain it without being interrupted and muddling things up. "... and we were just trying out the spell to unlock the door when you caught us," she finished.

"We know the room is supposed to be off limits, but we just wanted to know what was in there," Caiara chimed in. "We did wrong, and you're probably going to tell us not to keep meddling or throw us out or something, but we're so close to working it out!"

Glissia smiled softly. "Why would I stop you? You three have made far more progress in a matter of months than my first-circle priestesses and I have managed in years. Please, continue your research; I only ask that you let us in on whatever you may discover about the gateway device."

The three of them were stunned into

silence for a few moments. They had fully expected to be punished in some way, considering everything they had done. "So... we're not in trouble?" Soris asked tentatively.

"Well, you should make some reparations for borrowing my key without asking, and Arikele will probably have words with you for sneaking into her cupboard in the library, but I cannot punish you for seeking knowledge. That is what this place is for, after all."

Enkarini breathed a sigh of relief. She had not been looking forward to telling her father that her education at the Inner Library was over because she had messed up, and thankfully she would not have to. The other two had similar reactions, and they grinned at each other. "So how can we make up for taking your Archive key?" she asked.

Glissia looked at Soris. "Since taking the key was mostly, you're doing, it would be unfair to discipline the girls as well. Soris, as you enjoy copying things so much, you will spend the next few weeks making copies of the old temple records; some of them are becoming rather dilapidated and need renewing. You will do this in the evenings after your studies, and you will do it by hand." Soris groaned quietly. "Arikele will speak to you two," she said, looking over at Enkarini and Caiara.

The girls glanced at each other with twin grimaces. Arikele's punishment was likely to be far less pleasant than just copying some old records, but they would not complain. They were glad that this was all the punishment they were getting, and they would be able to keep researching the gateway.

"So, while you are in here, I shall divulge the knowledge we have gathered so far regarding the gateway. As you surmised earlier, Soris, the magic required to successfully open the doorway with the *asi-waju* spell is that known as Higher Magic, or Wyld Magic. Through long hours of study and practice, a select few of my priestesses have managed to develop another spell that counters the one locking the door, which they use to open it for study." Glissia took a large book from under the desk as she spoke and opened it to a page covered in untidy handwriting. "The last known Higher Mage,

Taliana the Wise, was the keeper of the gateway. She never attempted to open it, as far as we know, but she spent several years studying the device and left this book full of her notes and theories. As we were unable to read the Firsts' book that you found, we have been working with Taliana's notes. She mentions a diary a few times, possibly the one you have been working from?"

They glanced at each other before nodding. "That sounds likely," Caiara said.

"I thought so. Taliana was thought to be a direct descendant of Theresa Welldene, though it is impossible to confirm now. Our information on the Firsts is very sparse; I would like to read this diary at some point, once the translation is complete." She returned her gaze to the heavy tome before her. "During Taliana's examinations of the gateway device, she discovered at least three different types of magic contained within it; the kind that we now know as alchemy, that which we call Higher or Wyld Magic, and a third, unfamiliar type. From what you have said of the diary translation, this third type may be the dragon magic Astrid Torver describes. I believe there is a lot of study to be done, but with your inspired perspectives we may be able to work quicker now.

"These notes are quite comprehensive, but slightly jumbled. Taliana seems to have written down whatever came to her mind, in no particular order; from contemporary reports, she could be a little absent-minded at times. I believe I can trust you three to treat this with the respect it deserves. Perhaps it will assist with your studies," Glissia said, closing the book and handing it to Caiara, who was nearest to the desk.

The short-haired girl took it with trembling hands. "Thank you," she whispered. "We'll be ever so careful with it."

Glissia winked at them. "I'm sure you will. Maybe you could keep it in the secret space between shelves in the Archive," she suggested. "Soris can show you where it is."

"Wait, you know about that?" Soris cried.

"Of course. One does not become the high priestess of the knowledge goddess without knowing things," she replied as she ushered them out of the office. "Now, I suggest the three of you head home for the evening and start fresh tomorrow. Sleep works wonders for the mind."

~~~~~~~~~~~~~~~~~~~~~~~~~~~~~

Early evening sunlight blazed through the windows, making Jindara blink rapidly. She had called a general meeting in the town hall so that she could inform the people of Tewen what was happening with regard to the possible dragon attacks, and what she planned to do about them. Looking at the crowd in the hall, most of the town had come to the meeting, and she hoped they would be receptive to her idea. She rang the small bell kept in the main hall to quieten the crowd and command their attention.

"Thank you all for coming tonight; I am sure many of you had plans that have been interrupted, so I will not keep you too long. I have called this meeting to discuss a problem some of you may be aware of, namely the possibility that Tewen may soon be under attack. I have received a warning that the green dragons from the Grey Peaks to the north have become agitated and are flying south in a rage." She left out the fact that the warning had come from the Li Buqu; it would only cause panic to tell people that the lizard mages could break through the protective wards around the town.

Sceptical muttering swept through the crowd. "How do we even know these so-called dragons are real?" someone shouted.

Jindara pulled out one of Prince Michael's letters. "If you recall, almost three years ago we were visited by Prince Michael of Oakshire, who explained that dragons do exist, though they are not usually found in our lands. He had come here to search for the green dragons of his lands, who had left for reasons unknown," she reminded them all. "How and why these creatures have decided to fly around causing destruction is not relevant at this moment; my primary concern is how to defend this town. My husband is leading a group of mages who are trying to develop a shield over Tewen, but there is no guarantee it will be ready in time, or strong enough to fend off the dragons indefinitely. We have already had reports from some of the elven villages in the hills that great creatures have been seen in the skies."

"So, what can we do?" a woman in the

front called out.

Jindara gestured to two young men she had borrowed from the kitchens, who carried in a large roll of parchment. "I have received a letter from Prince Michael, detailing the kind of attacks we can expect from these dragons, and while it seems they are capable of causing devastation above ground, there is little they can do beneath it. I propose thay each family builds their own, small shelter in their gardens in which to take refuge from any potential attack." The two lads unrolled the parchment to reveal the design plans for the small dome shelters Jindara had thought of. "These can be sunk into the ground in your gardens, covered over with soil and protected from attack. We will provide the materials needed for the dome, and a list of suggested supplies to keep inside the finished shelter. It is possible that a prolonged attack will mean several hours inside them."

More muttering broke out, and Jindara waited for them to quiet. "We don't have a garden, where are we supposed to build one?" a man called out.

"I have already had some builders start

work on a large shelter beneath the Chief's Halls, for those of you who have no space to build your own. If you have the room, however, it is advisable to use it, as a shelter large enough to house the entire town would be a massive undertaking, and I do not believe we have enough time to complete one of that size. Of course, if you have a cellar in your home, you could shelter there; any secure underground structure ought to be sufficient protection for the types of attacks we can expect." Jindara unrolled the letter she still held. "According to the Prince, these dragons have magic that revolves around nature. Thankfully, most of their abilities are life-giving; they can make plants bloom and grow, influence certain animals, prolong the breeding seasons for creatures. The most problematic of their magic will be their weather controlling powers, which are apparently very strong, and their ability to breathe fire. He thinks it unlikely that they will use physical attacks, but their sheer size does make that a concern if they do choose to do so."

"What if this is all rubbish? We don't know for sure that these so-called dragons will even show up!" the disbelieving voice from before shouted. Some other voices started mumbling as well, sounds of confusion and dissent.

"There is a chance that this will not happen, yes," she told the assembled crowd. "However, I would rather be prepared for an attack that never arrives. If we make no preparations, and these creatures come with their fire and their magic, we stand little chance of repelling them. Our defences must be begun now so that they are ready." Most of the people she could see nodded at that; after the events of the last few years, many were keen to place caution first. "The materials for the shelters will be distributed over the next few days, and I would strongly recommend that you begin building yours as soon as you are able. We do not yet know how much time we have before the dragons arrive," she told them. "The building instructions are available tonight, if there are no more questions, we will pass them out; if any of your friends and neighbours are not here, take a copy for them and tell them what to expect."

Nobody else spoke up, so Jindara and the two kitchen lads each took a stack of instruction sheets and began distributing them through the crowd. As the townspeople began filtering out, she hoped that the shelters would be sufficient. Even more fervently, she hoped they would prove unnecessary.

~~~~~~~~~~~~~~~~~~~~~~~~~

Braklarn appeared in his study, Dekarem hanging from his arm. He lowered the other mage into a chair and sent a runner to fetch a healer, then turned back to his friend. "Before the healer gets here, can you tell me anything about this spell you mentioned?" He had very little experience with mind magic, so he wanted to know exactly what he was dealing with before trying to undo whatever damage had been done.

Dekarem seemed to have difficulty focusing, and his words slurred a little as he answered. "It's some sort of controlling enchantment. It links all the recruits' minds together as one, but it's possible to fight it. I've been trying, but the more minds get linked the harder it is to break away, like a magnet that keeps getting stronger and stronger. Distance helps me resist, that's one reason I tried to get out of Manak, but they came after me and I had to hide..." he clutched his head, screwing his eyes shut. "The farmer's son, he went to town, to buy a ring for his sweetheart; he took a cow, to sell in the town, to buy a ring for his sweetheart," he started to sing.

There was a brisk knock at the door, and Braklarn went to answer it. He could guess why Dekarem had started reciting children's rhymes; if he was trying to resist this mind-linking spell, it gave him something simple and unimportant to focus on. The healer could deal with the scrapes and bruises while he looked up something to help clear his friend's mind. He opened the door, and a large, dark skinned woman stood there who he recognised as a local healer. She didn't bother with small talk, immediately focused on the cuts on Dekarem's face and arms. She walked over and knelt beside him, pulling various pots and jars from her bag. "I'll be next door when you're finished," he told her. She nodded briefly, her attention on her patient. Braklarn grabbed his books on mind magic and left them to it.

About an hour later, the healer woman came in. "His body is healed, there were no major wounds and the larger cuts should heal within a day. He seems disturbed in the mind, though. I have little expertise in that area, would you have me send a fellow healer who does?" she asked.

"Thank you, but the trouble with his mind is magical, not medical. I believe I can help him myself in that regard," he replied as he marked a page in one of his books. He rose and gave the woman five gold coins. "For your service, and your rapid response to my call," he said. It was a vast overpayment for treating a few minor scrapes, but she had earned it by arriving so quickly, and he had always thought healers were underpaid. Most treated the poor for free, and while thanks and praise were fine things to receive, they did not put food on the table.

She thanked him and left, and he returned to the study. Dekarem was in the same chair, still singing faintly to himself. A few patches of gritty yellow paste covered some of his cuts. Braklarn pulled over the other chair and sat facing him, the book propped open on his knee. The spell he had found was a relatively simple one, at least in theory. The caster first had to rid his mind of all thoughts and feelings, to become totally calm and focused. Then he would make a link with the other person's mind, search for the connection caused by the other spell, break it and leave. He just hoped it would be as simple in practice.

He took a few moments to clear his mind, focus solely on his intent to break the spell that bound Dekarem to other minds, and carefully connected to the mind in front of him. The only other time he had tried this, with Remlika, he had experienced it as a dream-like state, his own mind providing images and sensations as it interpreted the connection with another. Then he had seen a large building, with each of its doors marked as things like 'childhood memory' or 'spell techniques'. This time, his own mind provided a similar kind of interpretation, except instead of a neatly ordered building, he was in a crowded and chaotic village square. People yelled, cried and laughed all around him, almost overwhelming him. These, he assumed, were representations of the other minds linked with Dekarem's; he ignored them and pushed through the throng, looking for something that could be the link between them. Thankfully they seemed to ignore him as well, though he suspected they would not be so obliging if they discovered what he was there to do. He spotted Dekarem a short distance away, struggling against several others who were trying to hold him back. Braklarn moved on, as freeing the image of his friend would likely have no effect other than to draw the attention of the rest.

He reached the edge of the crowd and found a loop of chain preventing further progress. This, he thought, must be the spell that bound them all together; he looked closer and saw thin lines of light connecting people to the chain. He returned to Dekarem, planning to get him to the chain before severing his connection to it. When he reached the struggling mage, the others who had been holding him were gone. Dekarem had sunk to the ground, clutching his head. Braklarn gently laid a hand on his arm. "I'm here to help. Follow me," he whispered into his friend's ear.

Dekarem initially resisted, but seemed

to recognise him and stood, and the two managed to slip back through the crowd to the chain. Braklarn could see the light connecting it to Dekarem clearly now, and he paused to think for a moment. If this were a real, physical situation, they would be able to simply slip under the chain to escape. Braklarn slowly crouched and waved an arm beneath the chain, and as his hand passed underneath it faded away, reappearing when he pulled it back. If he could break the connection with Dekarem, the two of them should be able to slide out of the bonds.

He was hesitant to use any magic here; it might attract unwanted attention, not to mention the potential risk of casting spells inside another person's mind. He pulled gently at the link, and it seemed to loosen slightly. A couple of the nearest people turned towards him, and he stopped until they looked away. This would have to be quick. He took a deep breath, seized the link and ripped it away from the chain.

The reaction was instantaneous; the entire crowd whipped around to face them, and the look in their eyes was of hateful madness. Dekarem seemed stunned, wobbling on his feet, and Braklarn grabbed him before he collapsed. He threw him under the chain, and the moment he hit the ground outside he disappeared. Hands reached out to grab him, and he acted without thinking. Fire erupted from his hands, and he sent streams of it at the people surrounding him. They shied away for a second, and he took the chance to duck under the chain himself.

As soon as he left the confines of the chain, he fell through a dizzying swirl of colour before opening his eyes again. He had returned to his study, Dekarem in the chair before him, looking a little dazed but otherwise fine. "I really, really do not want to go through that again," the other mage muttered. He lifted a hand to his forehead and seemed surprised to encounter a tangled mat of hair. "We are both out, aren't we?"

"I damn well hope so. That was insane," Braklarn replied. He stood, wavering slightly. "I've got a lot of things I want to ask you, but I think it can wait until tomorrow. Right now, all I want is a stiff drink or ten."

Dekarem also rose from the chair.

"Count me in. Anywhere but the Confused Duck."

Chapter Eight:
Through the Gateway

"Gods, how do those floors get so filthy?" Caiara exclaimed as she tried to wring the nearly black water from her shirt. "The first day, fine, I can see how there might have been a lot of dirt and dust accumulated. We've been at it for two weeks, surely there would at least be less dirt by now!"

Enkarini pulled yet another dried-up spider husk from her hair. "I'm pretty sure Arikele magics up more mess at the end of the day just to make sure we can't skip off home early. I must have dusted those shelves a thousand times, and I'm still finding cobwebs and dead bugs behind the books."

Caiara threw her a half smile. "At least you can use them in potions."

"At least it's over now," Enkarini said,

ignoring the comment. "She said until Eighth Day, and that's today, so we're done with scrubbing the library."

"You missed a spot," called Soris from the balcony. The girls looked up to see him smirking down at them. "Come on, I've been waiting ages."

They climbed up the stairs to meet him. "How's your punishment going anyway? Any more records fall apart in your hands?" Caiara teased him.

Soris pulled a face at her. "That only happened once," he protested. "Glissia says I've just got one more box to do now. I should be finished by next week."

"Good. I can't think of anything more boring than going through old accounts," Enkarini said. Initially, they had all wondered if the temple records Soris had to copy would be anything interesting or secret, but it had turned out they were only long lists of donations received at Talri-Pekra's shrines over the years. "Shall we get on, then?"

The other two nodded vigorously. "Definitely. I've been looking forward to this all week," Caiara said. "I can't wait to see if it works!"

Although Soris rolled his eyes at her over-the-top enthusiasm, he looked excited too, and it was hardly surprising. The three of them had spent all week in either the Archive or the gateway room, as they called it, trying to work out as much as they could about the magic contained in it, what it had been made from, and how to open it. They had passed on all they learned to Glissia and the other priestesses but had kept back one last secret; their research was not only for theory, they planned to actually try to open the gate. Tonight, would be the night, and they could barely contain themselves.

Enkarini opened the door, and the three of them piled in. The device stood in the centre of the room, lit by the hovering bluish globes that illuminated the rest of the Library. They always paused for a moment just to look at it; the unfamiliar metal of the pillars glimmered in the light, lending the whole setup a slightly unreal atmosphere. Enkarini didn't know if it was her imagination, but she thought she could feel the magic contained within the device.

"Shall we get started?" Caiara said,

moving towards the device. She pulled out the instructions they had so carefully translated and knelt beside one of the pillars. "I can almost feel this vibrating, you know. I think maybe it wants to be opened," she whispered.

Soris shook his head. "It's a pile of metal, Caiara. A pretty pile full of magic, true, but it's still just an object. It can't want anything."

The two girls shared a look. *This is why he can't grasp the more subtle magics,* Caiara thought to Enkarini. *He's got no appreciation for things he can't see and touch.*

It's not his fault. Most people only believe in what they can see, Enkarini replied. "Well, whatever the device wants or doesn't want, I want to open it," she said aloud. "So, how do we do this? It only takes one person to perform the opening spell, so which one of us should try it first?"

"I think we should figure out who has the best chance of making it work the first time. It sounds like something could go badly wrong if the caster messes up, so we should go with the best shot first," Soris suggested.

Caiara stood up. "So, who's got the best chance? We're all blood descendants of a First, however distantly, and we're all skilled in one area of magic or another," she said.

"Me," Enkarini mumbled. She looked up at the other two. "I'm not being vain or anything, but, well, judging by the spell to open the door, maybe it takes Wyld Magic to open the gateway as well. It's the only thing one of us can do that the other two can't," she told them.

They glanced at each other. "Sounds plausible," Soris said. "Are you absolutely sure you know what to do?"

She smiled. "We spent enough time reading over the instructions, I think I can remember what it said. Besides, you'll be standing right there to read them to me if I start to get anything mixed up," she said. "I'm not after taking all the glory, I just think it's the best chance we have of making this work."

"She's got a point," Caiara said thoughtfully. "We'll be right here, and if you think it's going wrong then just stop and get out," she told the younger girl.

Enkarini nodded, perused the instructions one more time, and stepped into the middle of the device. She wasn't imagining things; she could feel the magic buzzing all around her now. She took a second to gather herself, and gently grasped the thin strand of metal nearest to her. The buzzing seemed to intensify, flowing into her hands and through her whole body, making her feel as though she was a part of the structure. Slowly, she reached out and laid her other hand on the small sphere in the centre. It began to tingle under her fingers, and she waited a moment to be sure everything was connected properly. As she began to utter the incantation, the sphere started to vibrate, and somehow, she knew she had reached a point of no return; she would have to complete the ritual now.

She repeated the incantation, and the sphere shook violently, a few sparks flying from its surface and heat building in her hand. By the fourth iteration of the words, it was glowing white, with lightning flashing out of it to strike the five pillars surrounding her. She heard Caiara squealing, and knew it must look impressive from outside, but her attention was on the final repeat of the words. As soon as she had spoken the last syllable, the flashes ceased and the sphere froze, blinding white suddenly dulling to tarnished silver. She released both the sphere and the wire, quickly stepped out of the circle, and watched. It took a few seconds for the gateway to form fully, expanding from a small dot just above the sphere to a rippling, silvery oval large enough for a person to walk through.

"That was a bit scary," Caiara said. "Weren't you worried those lightning bolts were going to hit you?"

"Not really. It said the spell wouldn't harm the caster if they kept contact with the sphere, so I figured it would be fine as long as I just kept going," Enkarini replied. "What was it like watching?"

Caiara gave an exaggerated shudder. "Frightening. It was like you'd stepped into a storm cloud, there were flashes of lightning going everywhere and there was this weird smoky fog gathering around you. It was humming really loudly too, like it was all about to come to life or something."

Soris was busy examining the device. "Should we try to go through it, you think? I mean, what if whoever's on the other side is still as anti-mage as they were back then? We might not get a great reception," he said.

"Well we didn't go through all this trouble just to walk away now," Caiara told him. "Besides, that was hundreds of years ago, the people there probably don't mind magic anymore. We might even find the mages that stayed behind, I mean, their descendants."

While the two of them bickered, Enkarini had made her own decision to go and at least have a look around. She took a deep breath and leapt into the shimmering oval. She felt a brief jolt of static as she passed through, then a warm breeze on her skin. She seemed to be in some kind of valley, wildflowers scattered everywhere and the sun shining down. There were snow-capped mountains in a wide ring around the place, and a narrow, slightly overgrown path leading towards what looked like a small village some distance away. Soris stumbled into the back of her, his eyes shut tight, and Caiara spun gracefully through like a dancer.

"You can open your eyes now," she taunted the boy. "Stop acting like an ibikona."

Soris opened his eyes to throw a scowl in Caiara's direction. "Just because your nentila brain can't understand that a place we don't know anything about might be dangerous..."

Enkarini interrupted. "Quit it, you two. Anyone would think I'm the oldest one here, not the youngest," she told them. She liked both of them, but why couldn't they just be polite to each other? "Where are we, anyway?"

"I would assume we're in the valley Astrid described in her diary," Caiara said. "She mentioned that the one who stayed behind was going to start a settlement there, and that looks like a settlement to me." She pointed over to the cluster of buildings they could see in the distance.

"The diary also mentioned that it was the dragons' valley," Soris pointed out. "If it's the same one, shouldn't we be seeing a few dragons about?"

His words were almost prophetic. A

shadow swooped over them, and Enkarini looked up to see a familiar shape in the sky. She waved, thinking it was Maldor, and it dived towards them. As it got closer, she realised it was another, smaller black dragon, this one with cold grey eyes and tattered-looking wings.

It landed in front of them, looming above them with its sharp teeth bared. They drew back as one; Enkarini could tell this one was not as benevolent as Maldor. She could feel the other two trembling beside her as it lowered its head to peer at them. "What have we here?" it rumbled. "Three little children, so far from their homes. Is anyone missing them, I wonder?"

Another shadow landed behind this dragon, and Enkarini recognised Maldor's voice. "These are my wards, Sceadu. Leave this place." The smaller dragon turned, facing Maldor, who looked magnificent in the sunlight. "The Council hath banished thee for thy crimes. Wouldst thou call down further punishment by harming these innocents as well?"

Sceadu snarled. "The Council does not comprehend the greatness of my acts.

History shall remember me, but what shall become of thy name? Forgotten, thy legacy turned to dust and thy life as nothing in the wind." It took off, speeding away over the mountains.

"Thou hast chosen a poor time to visit, young sorceress," Maldor said, looking at Enkarini. "What brings thee and thy companions to these lands?"

She gestured back to the gateway, still open and glowing behind them. "We were studying the device on our side, and thought we'd try activating it," she started to explain.

Maldor smiled. "Then thou hast fulfilled a dream of thine ancestors, young one. Come, there is a village waiting to meet you," he said.

They began heading towards the village, almost jogging to keep up with the huge dragon beside them, though he was clearly moving as slowly as he could. Soris and Caiara seemed reluctant to speak, so Enkarini decided to fill the silence with a few questions. "What was that other dragon talking about? What's he done to get banished?"

"Sceadu has broken many of our laws. He has dabbled in many areas of magic, with little to no regard for the effects of his experiments on others. The Council finally acted, but too late. He shattered the veil between life and death, bringing devastation and ruin to the east," Maldor replied sombrely. "We are still working to contain the damage, but much of it is irreversible. The Shades are reluctant to return to their own realm, and they spread death to everything they touch."

Enkarini had no idea how to respond to that. Soris, however, had something to say. "You're telling us that another dragon raised the spirits of the dead, and now they're wandering about killing everything? Wow, I'm so glad we came here," he said.

"All places have their troubles, and we must deal with them as they arise," Maldor said. "Thine own lands are far from peaceful at this moment, I understand. Rest assured, this valley is likely the safest place for thou to be, as it is protected by the mages of Dragon's Teeth."

"Dragon's Teeth?" Caiara asked quietly.

241

"The name given to the village over yonder," Maldor told them. "Inspired by the surrounding mountains, long ago."

They continued in silence for a while, watching as the village became clearer. Enkarini wondered who lived there, and how they would feel about having the gateway open again.

~~~~~~~~~~~~~~~~~~~~

Crouched in the ruins of the old temple, Braklarn strained to hear any sounds leaking out of the basement. He and Dekarem had returned to the ruins of Manak after a lengthy talk about Gistran's plot to raise the god of Chaos. Apparently, there had been a hidden faction within the Creator's temple for decades, dedicated to the worship and raising of Chaos, which Braklarn felt explained a lot of the temple's actions. He had already worked out most of what was happening, but Dekarem's inside perspective had revealed a few vital facts.

Though the Chaos sect had hidden in the Creator's temple for such a long time, they had never managed to get any of their members so highly placed within the temple. Gistran was the perfect combination of three things; a follower of the Chaos cult, a mage willing to experiment with unknown magic, and capable of scheming his way to the position of High Priest. As far as Dekarem knew, Gistran had followed the path willingly, blinded by the lure of power and the favour of a god. It also seemed that this was part of a wider plan to raise several of the old gods, though Dekarem was not aware of any conscious collaboration between this sect and any of the others around. Whether the still-rising Mistress cult in Entamar was connected, he wasn't sure, but he suspected it might be.

"I can't hear a damn thing from here. We need to get in and take a look," he said to Dekarem.

Dekarem huffed. "If you get caught, I'm out of here. There's no way I'm going back under that spell," he warned.

Braklarn shook his head slightly and scrabbled through the rubble to the spot his friend had mentioned, where a concealed door led into the temple basement. Apparently, there were few security measures taken here, as there was nobody to secure the place against; Dekarem simply traced the spiral pattern on the door and moved back so that Braklarn could go first.

He crept down the gloomy passageway, freezing against the wall whenever he heard a voice or a movement he could not account for. Both men were under the concealment spell Braklarn had used before, so as long as they were careful, they should be able to pass undetected. The corridor was long and dingy, lit sporadically by flickering candles. A few doors were dotted along the walls, all closed. Braklarn paused to listen at a couple and heard nothing.

As the tunnel twisted and turned, sloping deeper into the ground, he heard the faint sounds of muttering from ahead and stopped to listen. There were two voices, one male and one female, but the words were unclear. He snuck closer, Dekarem trailing behind anxiously. A door at the end of the tunnel had a faint light shining under it, as though from a dying fire, and Braklarn cautiously pressed his ear against it.

"Over there, my dear," the man said. This close, the voice was recognisable as Gistran's. "We must ensure things are in place this time. A third chance may not be forthcoming."

"Yes, Your Holiness," the woman replied, her voice flat and monotonous. It sounded like Kolena, but Braklarn couldn't be certain.

He edged back around the last corner, to where Dekarem waited in the shadows. "It sounds like Gistran is setting something up; he mentioned that a third chance might not come, so this must be the second time he's tried whatever he's doing," he whispered. "I'm going to cast an eye and see if I can take a look in there."

"Don't let him spot it," Dekarem warned.

Braklarn nodded, and cast out a small, dim blue orb. He directed it along the floor, under the door and around the edges of the room. He immediately spotted Gistran, standing behind some sort of gilded stone altar. Luckily the priest's attention was on the young woman on the other side of the room. There was a tall cabinet of some sort behind the altar, which Braklarn sent his orb up the side of so he could get a better view of things. The woman turned from what she was doing, and he recognised Kolena, but her face was devoid of expression, as if she had been hypnotised or bewitched. Dozens of parchments had been pinned to the wall where Kolena stood, each depicting a face. Braklarn saw a few that were familiar, and with a jolt he realised they were the faces of the sacrificial victims. The altar held only a small bowl containing a little dark liquid, and a sharp silver knife. The spiral pattern had been drawn on the surface, and it glistened red in the flickering light.

"Can you see anything?" Dekarem hissed.

Braklarn allowed his magical eye to fade. "Kolena's in there, she's helping him set up some ritual items," he whispered back. "She looks like she's sleepwalking or something. Was she under the same spell as you?"

Dekarem frowned. "Maybe. I can't say I noticed her in the connection, but I don't really know her that well so I probably wouldn't have anyway."

"You need to take a look for yourself, maybe you'll see something I can't," Braklarn told him. "Recognise any of the items, or part of what they're doing."

With a heavy sigh, Dekarem cast out his own magical eye. He sent it along the same path as Braklarn's had taken, and for a few minutes they stood in silence. "The bastard's going to try raising the god again," he mumbled, a little louder than Braklarn was comfortable with. "He tried this back in Tewen a while ago. I was the one doing what he's bewitched Kolena into doing now, assisting with the set up. He used some beggar as the conduit that time though, and the poor sod died before the ritual completed."

"Conduit? What do you mean?" Braklarn asked.

"The waking ritual for the Chaos god needs a living conduit to provide life energy to the proceedings," Dekarem said shortly. "Basically, the god pulls himself through someone else in order to return. See, Chaos isn't sleeping as such, he's been cast out of this realm and trapped in another. The ritual to banish and bind him took a lot of black magic and human souls to complete, so it's going to take the same to reverse it."

Braklarn stood stunned for a moment.

"We have to stop it." He thought hard. "What were those pictures for? The faces of the victims pinned to the wall," he asked.

"Those are the trapped souls. He's bound the spirits of the victims to an image of their faces, so he can use them in the ritual. The spiral drawn on the altar is the anchor that he'll call the god to. The conduit lies on top of it, so her life can drain through to the god, giving him a connection to this realm. The knife is for making the mirror cut on the conduit's chest, so Chaos can pass through. He's already used the bowl, that's just something to hold her blood in while he paints the spiral," Dekarem explained quickly.

"Her? Does this conduit have to be female then?"

Dekarem threw him a look. "No, but this one is. He's going to use Kolena. I just saw her lying on the altar so he could check the positioning." Braklarn paled, started towards the door. "Hold it, he's not doing it now. If we go running in there, he'll just disappear and start over somewhere else. The ritual has to be done at sunrise, in the presence of seven faithful followers of

Chaos. Those followers aren't here yet, they're probably going to be arriving overnight. We can mess this up a lot more thoroughly if we wait for them to show and stop them reaching the ritual room, then we get in there and deal with him."

Braklarn struggled against his friend's grip. "If we grab Kolena now, he doesn't have a conduit and he can't do it anyway," he snapped back. "Or we could just take those pictures off the wall, then he's got no trapped souls to use. There are a lot of things we can do right now."

Dekarem dragged him back up the corridor. "Right, fine. We take away his conduit, or his trapped souls, or both. He notices they're gone, takes his loyal acolytes elsewhere, finds another conduit, traps more souls, and does the ritual next month instead of tomorrow. Moreover, we don't know where he's moved to or how to get there and stop him. I know she's your friend and you're worried about her. I know you want to put an end to this as soon as possible. But we. Need. To. Wait." They had reached the entrance to the passageway, and Dekarem held him against the wall. "I can't believe

I'm the one telling you to be patient."

Braklarn sagged. Dekarem's words made sense, but it didn't stop him wanting to just run in there and stop that mad priest before he could cause any more harm. "Fine. We'll wait until the morning. I'm not leaving, though. We wait right here and seize those damned Chaos acolytes as soon as they show up."

"That's fine by me," Dekarem agreed. "We can watch for them from that house opposite the old temple entrance, it looked like a good place to hide and it's got a pretty good view around the area."

~~~~~~~~~~~~~~~~~~~~~~~~~~~~

As they reached the outer edges of the village, they could see a small crowd had gathered. A tall woman with steel-grey hair and dark skin watched them curiously and stepped forward to greet them. "On behalf of my village, I welcome you here. Tell us, who are you?"

Caiara spoke first. "I'm Caiara, this is Soris and Enkarini. We've been studying the gateway in Slokos and we managed to open it," she said.

The woman inclined her head. "We

heard; ever since my ancestor Luke established this community, someone has watched the gate for signs of activity. I must admit, it is more of a tradition now than from any expectation that it would open again," she told them. "My name is Cassandra Miller; I am the mayor of Dragon's Teeth. Come, let me show you around."

Enkarini looked back at Maldor. "I shall fly back to my peaks, young one, and see thou on thy return to the gate." He took off, heading back towards the mountains, and she followed Cassandra into the village. The buildings they passed didn't seem to fit together at all, making the place seem as though shops and houses had been scooped up at random and just plonked together. Things started to look more coherent when they reached the centre of the village, and everything had a sort of magical feel to it. The buildings here looked old and settled, as though the stones had been there a long time already and planned on staying there for a long time to come.

Cassandra led them around the edge of a meadow where a small group of children played. Two older, one a girl with spiky pink hair and the other a dark, lanky boy, were chasing three smaller kids, two girls and a boy. Another pair of teenagers sat in the midst of a flower patch, a boy with glasses and dark, messy hair rapidly dousing the flames conjured by the girl with red hair and ashen skin. "My grandsons, Martyn and Edwin," Cassandra told them, pointing to the lanky boy and the smaller, similar boy being chased. "I'm sure you'll have the opportunity to meet them some time. Come," she said, beckoning them into a large hall that looked like a castle from a story book.

They followed her through the hall and into a small, ornate meeting room. A large painting of a dark-skinned, kind faced man hung on the far wall, and Enkarini was strongly reminded of Remlik. Six people sat around the table, watching the new arrivals closely as they took seats along the end. Cassandra sat at the head, under the portrait, and smiled at them.

"Allow me to introduce the council; our own equivalent to that of the dragons." She gestured to the olive-skinned woman nearest to Caiara. "Alessa Willow, the headmistress of the school."

Alessa nodded and winked, hazel eyes twinkling in the light. "Pleased to meet you."

"Luke Forester, in charge of all non-magical matters," Cassandra continued, and the round-faced man next to Alessa grinned. "My son Jonathan, the deputy mayor," she nudged the sleepy man on her right. "At least he is when he's awake," she scolded.

Jonathan rolled his shoulders, groaning slightly. "You know I've been up all night trying to deal with this veil thing." He nodded absently at the three of them.

Cassandra looked down the other side of the table. "This is Saffron Clarke, who assists any new arrivals in settling," the blonde, freckled woman smiled, "and Malise Blackwood, who runs the magical research facility on the far side of town."

The messy-haired woman in a long white coat gave them a little wave. "I would love to hear how magic has progressed and changed in your lands."

"And of course, our head of law enforcement, Ustin Fogsbaine." The man nearest to Soris nodded slowly, his eyes fixed on them. He was dark-haired and pale, with glittering black eyes and an oddly angular bearing. Enkarini figured he was in charge of law keeping because nobody would dare to cross him. "So, how did you come to open the gateway that has been sealed for so long?" Cassandra asked them, leaning forwards.

They glanced at each other before once again telling the story, though they gave a few more details than they had told Glissia. After all, it was unlikely that these people would be terribly cross with them, since they had not broken any rules here yet.

"Fascinating," Malise murmured when they finished. "You say casting and alchemy have diverged from one another? I wonder why... and that mages need to practise extreme focus in order to cast... I suppose it could be an effect of the magical blood diluting over the years..." she trailed off, clearly lost in some theory the rest were not privy to.

Caiara leant forwards. "I have a question; why has nobody here attempted to open the gateway? Surely it would have been easier from this side, if you can all do Wyld Magic."

All heads turned to Cassandra. "As I am sure you know, in order to open the gateway, one must be a blood descendant of the original mages who first activated it. The only one of the groups who remained here to continue the line was Luke Miller, and he saw fit to seal the device so that it was impossible to reopen from this side," she told them. "The prevailing opinion among non-mages at the time was that all magic users were wicked, devilish creatures. He knew that if word reached the kingdom that the mages had fled to a new land, there would be those who wished to follow and cause harm, so he ensured that there would be no way for them to do so."

"Well, then why not just destroy the device on this side?" Soris asked.

"That would have left the device on your side useless as well," Malise answered. "The few who stayed here still hoped that the others would find some way to reach them, or to bring them through without having to leave the gate open. Without a device at both ends, there would have been no hope of that."

Enkarini suddenly thought of something. "Wait, how did the device on our side get there in the first place then? If whatever spell they used to open the gateway needed one at both ends, how did they get there to put one there, to get there with?" She paused at the end, trying to work out if what she had just said made any sense.

Alessa smiled at her. "Our ancestors asked for help from the dragons, who had acted as both teachers and protectors for many years beforehand. Their magic is far more powerful than our own, even now, and they were able to cross the world to place the second device. The silver and gold dragons who made that journey chose to remain in the new land, I believe," she explained. "We haven't heard anything of them since; perhaps you can tell us what happened to them?"

They all shook their heads. "The only dragons we've heard about are green ones," Enkarini said. "I don't know anything about silver or gold ones."

"Enough talking; this isn't supposed to be a history lesson," Ustin suddenly declared. "Let's see what you three can do," he said.

The rest looked to Cassandra for confirmation. "I suppose it is a little stuffy in here," she said, rising from her seat. "And I'm sure there will be ample time to discuss things at a later date. Perhaps we can also show you the kind of magic we teach here, while we're outside."

They filtered back out to the meadow, where Luke and Alessa ushered the playing children to one side. "So, let's see your most impressive skills, then we can give you a demonstration of ours," Alessa said once a large enough space was cleared.

Never one to miss a chance to show off, Soris stepped forwards. "I'm good at a lot of things, but my best spells are fire spells," he said with a smirk. Flames sprung from his hands and licked up his arms, and he spent at least five minutes making them dance and whirl around him. He ended his display by forming the fire into a huge dragon, which soared overhead before vanishing in a puff of smoke. The children watching clapped and whooped excitedly.

"Well controlled; fire can be a tricky

thing to work with," Saffron told him. "I suspect my niece will want to talk with you. She shares your love of flames," she nodded to the ashen girl they had seen earlier, who had watched Soris with a keen interest throughout. "How about you?" she asked Caiara.

The blonde girl started. "My real talent is Seeing, which doesn't look as impressive as that. I suppose I could..."

"Past, present, or future?" Jonathan interrupted.

"Um, all of them, though not all at once," Caiara said.

He walked across to her. "Okay, then read me. Anything about my life," he said.

"Right." She let her eyes close halfway, drifting into a trance. "You have a scar on the right side of your chest, from when you were nine. You had climbed to the top of the big oak tree to impress Fiona Gates, but she wasn't even watching. You slipped and fell because it was raining, and a branch broke and went through your side. Saffron ran to get Mr Wilson to heal you, and your mum grounded you for a month afterwards, but you secretly didn't mind because you were too embarrassed to go outside anyway," she told them.

He nodded, clearly impressed. "She's good. Any other talents?"

"I can do other spells but not amazingly well. Rini's been teaching me alchemy and trying to show me how to summon a cloud, but I haven't got the hang of that yet," she replied.

"Summon a cloud? As in weather magic or...?" Malise asked.

Enkarini ducked her head shyly. "Maybe I should just show you," she said. She moved into the centre of the space and took a moment to call up her black cloud. It appeared almost instantly, swirling around her like a thick, dark fog. For a few moments, she simply let it float there, and then she began to manipulate it. "I haven't been practising this bit for long," she called to them. She made it into a few simple shapes, which drew some 'oohs' from the kids watching, and tried to separate it into two parts, but it dissipated at that point, leaving her blinking in the bright sunlight.

"Very good. For someone your age to have that level of control over raw magic is remarkable," Ustin told her. "How long have you been able to summon like that?"

She thought back. "About a year, maybe a little longer. I didn't realise I was doing it the first few times," she said.

He exchanged a look with Malise. "I would like to talk with you at some point, young lady. Inherent, unconscious talent like yours is quite rare."

"Another time, perhaps. We did promise a demonstration of our own," Cassandra reminded them. "Shall I begin?"

The next half hour was spent watching the five Council mages show off their command of the elements; Cassandra began with a spectacular array of ice spells, which left the meadow covered in frost until Saffron thawed it with her fire magic. Malise and Ustin worked together to call up a fierce storm, with thunder that shook the earth and lightning crackling across the whole sky. Alessa finished the display, summoning up her own cloud of raw magic to heal the grass and flowers, leaving the meadow as calm and pretty as it had first looked.

By this time most of the small town

seemed to have gathered to watch, and all applauded the five who had performed. "Of course, we have all been practising these skills for many years," Cassandra said as the rest went to speak with members of the crowd. "If any of you should choose to stay here and learn, you would be most welcome."

Enkarini looked at the other two. Soris seemed hesitant, and Caiara looked very tempted by the offer, as she was herself, but she didn't want to just abandon her own life either. "Maybe... I don't know if I could just leave my family like that, though. If I go home for now, could I come back some time?" she asked.

Cassandra smiled gently. "You certainly could. Perhaps that would be the sensible course of action for all of you; the gateway will always be open to you, if you wish to return here." She glanced up towards the sky, which had darkened considerably in the short time they had been outside. "Night is almost upon us. Shall I call Maldor to escort you back?"

"I think we can find our own way back to the gate," Soris said. "It's not exactly hard to find." He pointed eastwards, where a faint silvery glow was visible in the sky.

Caiara nudged him. "What if that other dragon comes back, though? The one that wanted to eat us or whatever?"

"I can call him, I think," Enkarini said. She wasn't quite sure, but she had a feeling that Maldor's arrival shortly after they stepped through the gateway was no coincidence. "Thank you for everything, I'm sure we'll see you again."

Cassandra nodded. "I hope so. I shall walk to the edge of the town with you," she said, leading them back down the path they had followed earlier. Small, twinkling lights emerged to dance overhead as they walked, flitting between the pools of soft light cast by the lanterns along the way. "The autumn is the most wonderful time of year, in my view," she said as they reached the end of the trail.

"Autumn? It's midsummer tomorrow," Caiara said.

"In your lands, perhaps. Remember, we are on opposite sides of the world; it would follow that the seasons differ between our homes," Cassandra told them. She looked upwards, and a great black shadow swooped towards them. "It appears there is no need to call Maldor after all." Enkarini smiled when he landed. She had begun to think of the black dragon as a friend, although they had only met a handful of times.

They bade farewell to Cassandra and followed the dragon back towards the gateway in a thoughtful silence. They paused before stepping through and looked back towards the small town. "I think... yes, I'm going to come back here, someday soon," Caiara said softly. "There's a lot to learn here and I want to learn it."

"Thou art welcome to return, young one," Maldor told her. "Thou also," he said with a nod to Soris.

"I'll think about it," the boy replied quietly. "We've got things to do at home first, though." With a nod to the great dragon, Soris stepped back through the gateway. Caiara reluctantly followed, still gazing over her shoulder at the town.

Enkarini hesitated. "Maldor, I... I wanted to ask something," she began. "When Alessa summoned up her cloud, it wasn't all black and smoky like mine, it was green. How come?"

"Alessa Willow has a strong aptitude for nature magic, which reflects in the colour of raw magic she can summon," he said. "I believe young Ember Clarke summons a red cloud, as she has affinity with the fire magics. The hue and shade of one's raw magic summoning is merely a representation of one's own abilities and talents."

Enkarini gazed forlornly at her hands, barely seeing them as Maldor's words bounced around in her mind. "So, it is black magic," she whispered. "Aila was right. I am a dark sorceress."

"Of course not," the dragon scoffed. "Dark and light, good and evil; these are words humans apply to magic for their own convenience. Many 'evil' magics are only called such due to lack of ability or understanding. Thy kind often find it simpler to forbid something and call it 'dark' than learn how to use it safely." He lowered his head to meet her eyes. "Fret not, young one. We can show thee how to use thy talents. Thou can then use them any way thou choose. As a knife can be used to slice bread or flesh, so can magic be used for both kind and cruel purposes. It does not matter what 'type' of magic it is, for all is magic."

"But..." Enkarini looked up at him, trying to find the words to express what she felt.

Maldor blinked slowly. "If thou must label this, we refer to it as Shadow magic, or Spirit magic. While others are skilled in the manipulation of the physical, Shadow magic deals with the less tangible; it lends force and presence to that which otherwise cannot be seen."

Enkarini was still unsure. "I don't know what you mean," she said.

"Then thou must learn and understand thy gifts," he rumbled. "If ever thou hast need, call upon me and I shall come to thine aid. Now, thy friends await thee on the other side." He straightened up, stretching his wings out. "Until we meet again, young sorceress."

She waved absently, still lost in her thoughts, and stepped back through the gateway. Thankfully the room was empty aside from Soris and Caiara, and the three of them wished each other goodnight without further discussion. It had been a very long night, and anything they wanted to talk about could wait until morning.

~~~~~~~~~~~~~~~~~~~~~~~~~~~~~~

"The damage above ground is severe, Chief, but almost all of the citizens of Akram were saved. Those without shelters were evacuated to the outlying farms; the great beasts seem to be moving in a straight path rather than targeting any particular place," the messenger reported. "Chief Onkadal wishes you luck in defending your town and has sent a troop of his best men to assist your own army. They should arrive within a day."

Jindara ran a hand through her hair. "Then much of Akram will need to be rebuilt again," she muttered. "Thank Chief Onkadal for his report, and for sending us extra soldiers. I will repay him by sending my best builders to help with the work when this is over," she told the messenger. The young boy bowed and jogged out of the hall, leaving Jindara to her own thoughts.

She knew many of the townspeople had already completed their shelters, but a lot had not even started yet. She would have to tell people that they had only hours to finish their domes, or else find a place underground to wait out the attack. She knew the temples of Ralor-Kanj and Dranj-Aria had opened their own cellars, but they could not hold everyone who was currently shelter-less. Her own large basement had been completed only yesterday, which would hold around a hundred people, but even that would leave several families unprotected. She would have to alert everyone quickly, try to ensure that as many people as possible got their shelters up within the day.

The army had been drilling almost constantly for a month, preparing for any sort of aerial attacks that could possibly come their way; she wrote a hasty note to her generals to tell them to increase watches and expect attack by tomorrow. She just hoped people would heed the warnings. Tomorrow was supposed to be the day of the midsummer feast, but she had postponed it because of the approaching dragons. Everyone had complained, of course; the midsummer feast had never been cancelled, or even moved, in living memory. She had placated the town with the promise of a double feast for the adulthood ceremony at the end of summer, and thankfully a mass revolt had been averted, but there were still whispers of small street parties being organised around Tewen.

Jindara lifted herself out of her chair and headed for the main doors. The markets and streets should still be crowded, as sunset was still a few hours away. She would make a hasty speech in the main market square and hope that enough people heard and listened. Just before she left, her maid Mishina came running over to her. "Chief, I heard some of the kitchen girls talking just now, they're saying we're going to be attacked in the morning," she said. "Everyone's worried but they're too scared to come and ask, so I thought I should see what's happening." She tilted her head inquisitively, watching Jindara closely.

"I'll speak to everyone shortly and explain in more detail but tell them all not to get in a panic," Jindara said. The last thing she needed was her own staff rioting and causing mass hysteria. "We have known for weeks that there was a possibility of attack, and I have just been told it is a certainty. I expect it will be within a day or two, at most, but as long as you have all prepared properly, I see no reason for anyone to be too concerned. Try to calm everyone, I will hold a meeting with the staff when I return."

Mishina nodded, her fluffy brown hair bouncing around her face. "Thank you, Chief. I thought you'd have it all under control," she said. "I'll tell everyone to keep calm and wait for you to speak to them." She smiled and walked back towards the kitchens.

Jindara watched her go, then turned back to the doors. She hoped the rest of Tewen would be as receptive as Mishina had been.

Chapter Nine:
The End

The inky sky had just begun to lighten when the first acolyte arrived. Braklarn nudged Dekarem sharply in the ribs and pointed towards the man climbing over the rubble that littered the old square. With a grim nod, the two men rose and moved towards the newcomer. The plan was to incapacitate whatever acolytes they caught, which would prevent Gistran performing the ritual as needed, and then head back down to the chamber themselves and deal with the priest.

Braklarn quickly cast a freezing spell at the acolyte, stopping him in his tracks. Dekarem dragged him back into the ruined house and tied him to a beam. "How many do you suppose are coming?" he muttered, keeping watch while his friend worked the stiff rope into knots.

"Probably about a dozen have been asked to come," Dekarem whispered back. "If he needs seven for the ritual it would make sense to call for more, that way if a few are delayed or whatever he should still have enough there to go ahead."

They resumed their watch, each staring out of opposite sides of the walls. After a few minutes, three men arrived at once, walking together. Braklarn cursed softly, unsure of how to do this without raising the alarm. Dekarem gave him a look, and muttered, "follow my lead."

Braklarn watched as he crept out of the old house, around to a spot behind the three acolytes, and hailed them. They all turned and paused. "What are you doing here? I heard you'd abandoned us," one of them said.

Dekarem shrugged. "You can't believe everything you hear; you know. His Holiness asked me to attend the waking ceremony."

Realising what the plan was, Braklarn snuck up behind them while the other mage kept them talking. He silently stunned one of them, holding him up with a levitation spell, and froze a second one. The one Dekarem was talking to noticed something was up with his companions and span around to see Braklarn holding them under spells. He yelled, and Dekarem quickly silenced and froze him from behind. They got the three into the house and bound them alongside the first, then paused for a moment.

"That was close. What if more of them show up together?" Dekarem asked. "These three fell for it, but some of Gistran's favourites are a lot cleverer than them. I don't know if I'll be able to distract the others like that," he said.

Braklarn shook his head. He had no idea how they were going to grab the rest of the acolytes... "Damn," he said. "How did they slip past?" He pointed across to the concealed entrance, where a group of four people were just entering.

Dekarem cursed. "We can't let any more get in there. Let's hide this bunch and move closer, they might have come in from the other side of the temple."

They hid the unconscious acolytes under an old sheet they had found and crept through the rubble to a point near the doorway. For almost an hour, they waited in silence for any new arrivals, but none showed. The sky steadily lightened above them, and Braklarn started to fret. "It's almost sunrise, where are the rest of them?" he whispered harshly.

Dekarem only shrugged. "Maybe we should just go in. It's about time to start the ritual, so whatever's happening now, we'll need to be down there to do anything about it."

Braklarn nodded, a sick feeling rising in his throat. They had probably been spotted, or maybe one of the acolytes had worked out that four had gone missing and alerted Gistran. They rushed down the passageway to the room at the end and heard chanting from within. Braklarn hit the door, expecting it to fly open and at least cause a distraction to interrupt the ritual, but it held fast. "They must have locked it," he said, cursing the mad cult.

"Stand back," Dekarem instructed, conjuring a massive fireball to blast the door away. It blistered and charred, but still would not open. The freshly shaven mage swore violently. "Try transporting in," he suggested.

Braklarn tried but encountered some sort of block. "There must be a ward up, I can't get through," he said. The chanting from inside had built to a crescendo, and they could hear flapping, rattling sounds like parchment caught in a high wind. Growing desperate, he started blasting the door with anything that came to mind; fire, ice, lightning, whatever could break through the wards holding it closed. Dekarem was doing the same beside him, and eventually the wood splintered into pieces, revealing the madness inside.

The seven acolytes stood in a semicircle below the altar, screeching their chant at the ceiling. Gistran stood behind it, the knife in his hand and a demented look in his eyes. "Too late, boys! Our lord rises!" he shrieked.

Kolena hovered above the altar, covered only in a thin white sheet that was stained with red. A pulsing, sickly yellow light surrounded her, and the parchment images whirled around like leaves in a cyclone. One by one, the faces burst into flames, leaving a swirl of ashes in the air.

Braklarn tried to push forwards, to do something, anything to stop this ritual. He found himself straining against a solid block of air, though; apparently the wooden door had given way, but the ward had not. Abruptly, the light vanished and Kolena fell from the air, flopping over the altar like a ragdoll. The acolytes ceased their chant and fell to their knees in supplication, Gistran bowed low as a form coalesced in the centre of the room.

It appeared as a young man of average height, with dark brown hair and a barrel chest. He seemed to examine himself, turning slowly on the spot. "At last. I was starting to think my followers would never return me to my rightful realm," he said.

Gistran appeared to smile at the floor. "The ones who banished you did not make it simple to reverse their bindings," he replied softly. "But there will always be those of us who seek out chaos."

The young man cocked his head, looking around at the doorway. "There are also those who seek to prevent me," he said, glowing yellow eyes fixed on the two mages pressed up against the wards. "Still, sometimes I win. Come, we have things to do." He snapped his fingers, and he, Gistran and the seven acolytes vanished in a flash.

Braklarn toppled forwards and staggered to catch himself. "Kolena," he muttered, running across to the limp young woman. He leant close, listening for a breath or heartbeat. "She's alive, but only just."

"Good. We can get her to a healer," Dekarem said. He was standing by the shelf at the back of the room, staring at some sort of scroll worked metal disc. "First we need to destroy this. It's the anchor for the mind link spell. If she's under it, she might heal but she'll just try to get back to him."

"Any ideas?" Braklarn said. Something buzzed in his pocket, and he pulled out a small crystal. It was something he had discovered in one of the Li Buqu books some time ago, a device that allowed short, simple messages to be transmitted between a pair. He had given the other half of this pair to Jindara, so she would be able to contact him quickly if he was away without a calling mirror. "Something that won't take too long, preferably."

In answer, Dekarem threw the disc to

the ground and cast lightning at it until it shattered. "Not delicate, but it should break the spell." Kolena shuddered on the altar, cried out faintly, and her eyes flickered open for a second. "See if she still looks brainwashed."

Braklarn leant over, peering into Kolena's eyes. She seemed unfocused and weak, but not blank as she had been before. "I think she's out of the spell. She needs healing, but Tewen's about to be attacked. Get her to Astator, and find a good healer," he instructed. "Once she's safe, I'll need you to come join me. If we're going to keep the shield in place for any decent length of time, we'll need all the mages we can get."

Dekarem reluctantly nodded, picked up Kolena and laid her across his shoulders, and vanished. Braklarn looked around the ritual chamber, disgusted with himself for letting Gistran escape. At least they had managed to break the spell that bound the bewitched followers, which was something, he supposed. It would take time for Gistran to build up that network again, and he hoped to get some sort of warning out before the priest got too far. What they were going to do about the reborn Chaos god, he had no clue, but that would have to wait until another day. He set a raging fire before transporting back to Tewen; if nothing else, it would leave this ritual room unusable for the future.

~~~~~~~~~~~~~~~~~~~~~~~~~~~~~~

Enkarini spun faster and faster, spurred on by the music and the almost infectious joy that filled the atmosphere in the street. Though this was not an official feast, it seemed that even a looming threat of attack could not stop people celebrating midsummer. Chief Jindara had decided to postpone the official midsummer feast until the green dragons had been dealt with, which had resulted in several small parties being held throughout Tewen. Harndak had told both of them to wait for the official feast, but when a group of their neighbours had set up a table of food and begun dancing in the street outside, they had all been enticed to join in the fun.

Some of the other children in the street had mentioned a bigger party with more food a few streets over, and both Caiara and Enkarini had been tempted by the promise of a huge syrup cake that one boy swore he'd seen there. They had all crept away, and sure enough there was a long table simply covered in cakes and pastries, so heavily laden that it was almost collapsing under the weight. Both girls had grabbed a huge slice of the coveted syrup cake, and after getting thoroughly sticky they had started dancing to the wild drum beat that echoed off the houses around them.

The beat suddenly changed, a more frantic, distant drumming that threw off the musicians' rhythm. They ground to an erratic halt, and the partiers looked around, hearing the whistles of the watchmen now the music had stopped. "Attack! Attack!" came the cry from the walls, repeated by others as it worked its way through the town. A few people started filtering into their homes, the sensible ones retreating to their shelters. Enkarini looked around for her father but couldn't see him anywhere. She remembered they had left him back in their own street when they snuck off to this party.

"Remain calm, and go to your shelters and cellars," came a deafening, distorted voice, cast across the town with magic.

"Soldiers and mages are to report to the market square for defence duty. All others must seek out underground shelter, ensure your family is safe." The message repeated, sending everyone into a frantic rush.

Enkarini found herself jostled and carried down the street with a group of smaller children, and lost Caiara in the panic. She managed to extricate herself before they piled into a house, and sought out her friend, but she was nowhere to be seen. She wasn't even sure how to get back to her own street from here, everything looked different somehow, though she had probably walked down this road dozens of times there had never been this much frightened activity around. People shouted and screamed, banging on doors and begging to be let into their neighbours' shelters.

She edged down a side street, looking for a quiet place where she could focus. Harndak had dug them a shelter in the back garden as soon as the materials had been delivered, so she knew they had a safe place to go while the army sorted out the attack, but she didn't know how to get home from here. She found herself at the back of a tailor's shop and leant against the wall tiredly. "Where am I?" she muttered to herself. She didn't remember a tailor anywhere near home and was reluctant to wander aimlessly in this mass panic.

An image of Maldor suddenly popped into her head, and she wondered if she ought to try calling him. He had said that if she was in need of help, she could call him, and she definitely needed help right now. *How can I call him, though?* she thought. There was no time to gather ingredients and perform the calling spell like she had before.

I hear thy call, young one. What is thy need? The deep voice seemed to roll through her mind, drowning out the noise and yells around her.

She sighed in relief. *My home is being attacked by the green dragons, I'm stuck outside and can't find my way home,* she thought back.

We shall assist. Protect thyself as best you can, he replied after a moment's pause. *We will endeavour to arrive quickly.*

Enkarini blinked, the image of the black dragon fading from her mind. The street she had come from had filled with smoke in the short time she had been standing there, and it blew down her little alley, making her cough. She stumbled away from it, into another street, and pushed through the frantic, panicked people that were running back and forth shouting and screaming. She found a post that usually held a lantern, and clung to it tightly, hoping Maldor would not take too long to come.

~~~~~~~~~~~~~~~~~~~~~~~~~~~~~

Jindara ran back to the Halls to open the shelter for the townspeople. She had been organising the troop of soldiers from Akram when the alarm drums sounded and had had to leave them under the command of one of her generals. She knew the shelter under her Halls would not be large enough for everyone, too many people had been complacent about their own shelters and would now have nowhere to go. She would have to prioritise; children and mothers with infants would have to be the first in, and if there was no room for the rest then so be it. There was already a crowd building when she arrived, she quickly guessed there were about a hundred and fifty there. "Right, I want this organised properly!" she called to them all. "Young children, mothers and infants in first, no exceptions!"

The crowd shuffled about to let the children through, accompanied by women who carried babies. They filed in quickly, through the Halls and down into the large empty basement the workers had dug. The space rapidly filled, and Jindara could see there was very little room left already. She quickly assessed the crowd remaining and decided to let them in; it would be uncomfortable, but they would be fine for a few hours. "Right, the rest of you proceed calmly; you'll have a cramped few hours, but you'll be safe," she told them. The men and remaining women followed the children through, and Jindara shut the doors of the Halls. Once the crowd had entered the shelter, she ran to fetch her own daughter.

Larinde was staring out of the window in the nursery, her eyes fixed on the green shapes in the sky. "Mama what?" she cried, pointing at them.

Jindara lifted her off the floor and hushed her. "Nothing that's going to hurt you, sweetie. Come on, we're going to have a little adventure now. Remember Mama had those men digging to make a big room? We're going to go play there for a while," she said, trying to keep the child calm.

"Dada there?" the little girl asked.

Jindara stopped for a second. "Dada will be there later, right now he's got things to sort out. There are lots of other children there though, you can play and make new friends," she explained. She had just reached the main hall when her maid Mishina ran out of the kitchens. "Chief, there's a big crowd out the front and they're panicking," she said. "I think they want to get in the shelter, I tried saying there wasn't room but they won't listen..."

"I'll speak to them," Jindara interrupted. She glanced out of the window, seeing the shapes in the sky coming closer. It felt wrong to hide underground and leave her people to face this danger without their Chief. Jindara gave her daughter one last hug. "Mishina, take Larinde and get into the shelter. I have to do my duty," she said grimly.

The young maid who had helped her through birthing took the child from her arms. "We'll see you when this is over," she whispered, tears sparkling in her sea-green eyes. She fled to the shelter, and Jindara heard the door slam shut behind her. She took a deep, slow breath to calm herself before marching out of the side door of the Halls and looking over at the frightened, angry crowd that had gathered outside.

Everyone yelled and screamed at once, making it hard to hear any one protest in the cacophony. "The shelter here is full! There is no more room; find cellars, basements, anywhere underground that you can!" she shouted over to them. There was nothing else she could tell them, and she hoped they would listen, or at least scatter throughout the town so that the dragons would not have such a huge target.

"You can't just leave us out here!" she heard someone screaming. As she turned away, Jindara tried to blank it all out; the shelter at her Halls was overfull already, and if she opened the doors again now everyone would try to pile in, and people would be crushed in the stampede. She had given these people plenty of time to build their own families a shelter, and despite her warnings they had chosen not to. They would have to take their chances like she was.

She could see Braklarn on a roof nearby with a group of other mages, desperately trying to reinforce the shield over the town. Part of her wanted to call out to him, declare her love and support, but he thought she was in the shelter with their daughter, and if he knew she was not he would be unable to focus fully on his task. With a knife digging into her heart, she turned away, refusing to think that it could be the last time she laid eyes on her husband. The army was assembling in the market square, and she made her way through the streets to join them. Every extra bow would help now.

The officers were barking orders when she arrived in the square. The battalion from Akram had already marshalled and begun to move out, heading towards the north side of the town. She approached the nearest commander and saluted. "Where do you need me?"

He blinked, obviously confused. "Chief, I didn't expect to see you here," he said. "Aren't you taking shelter with your family?"

Jindara shook her head. "My daughter is safe, that is all that matters. My place is protecting my town and my people. So, where do you need me?" she asked once more.

"There's a squadron of archers heading over to the west side, Chief. The plan is to try and divert the beasts around the western edge of town, since it's less densely inhabited," the commander told her. "If the gods are with us, we can push them around the outside of the town, but if they do fly over us then at least there are less people living that side."

She interpreted that as 'less people in danger' and silently approved. "Then I shall join the archers on the west side. May the gods be with you, Commander."

The man saluted her and returned to his own soldiers. Jindara crossed the square to join the archers heading west, seizing a bow from the munitions tent as she passed it. The weapons were almost all gone, and she was lucky to get a full quiver to go with her bow. The squadron moved out a moment later, pushing their way through the streets that seemed full of running, shouting people. The leader of the troop tried to send people back to their homes, or into their cellars or neighbours' basements, but there was too much panic in the air. Jindara looked up and saw the vast green shapes swooping over the town. There were eight of them, all flying in a line towards the centre of Tewen, and the archers around her raised their bows.

"Draw them this way, men!" the commander shouted. A volley of arrows sped towards the dragons, and several of them struck home. The ones that had been hit shook themselves, and the formation broke. They continued to lead a couple out towards the western side of town, but the rest had scattered across the sky.

A loud chorus of screams rose from a street to the left, and Jindara looked over to see three more dragons approaching; these were red, blue and black ones, however, and seemed to ignore the people below them in order to launch themselves at the green ones. She turned to the troop commander. "Don't attack those three, I think they're here to help," she said. She wasn't sure where they'd come from, but she recalled Prince Michael telling her that the rest of the dragons in the north were trying to help, somehow. Perhaps he had managed to persuade some of them to come and help the People in their time of need.

She lost track of time for a while, occupied only with the present of terrified people and shaking earth, green fire rampaging through the streets and destroying buildings. The squadron seemed to fracture and disband, leaving her and two others walking the streets alone. A huge crash rang through the town, and she caught herself praying that it had been nothing too devastating. She heard cheers, which left her thoroughly confused, until one of the archers she had stuck with shouted out. "One down! I don't know how, but one of the beasts is down!"

"Where?" she demanded.

He grinned beneath his overlarge helmet. "Down there, Chief, and that blue one's doing something to hold it down. You were right about them being here to help out."

Jindara couldn't help but smile in

return; the man's grin was contagious. "Excellent. That leaves seven to deal with," she said. "Let's hope we can manage it."

~~~~~~~~~~~~~~~~~~~~~~~~~~~~~~~

Enkarini clung to her post, shouting for her father and Caiara, but her cries were lost in the screams of those around her. Someone staggered out of nowhere and grabbed hold of her, shouting hysterically about death and wrath, wrenching her away from the pole. She pulled herself out of the crazed woman's clutches and quickly scrambled down a side street, emerging into the market square, where the few stalls that had been out were abandoned and collapsing. A couple of military tents stood in the centre, unattended and empty, where the army had clearly marshalled and moved out earlier.

Hearing screams from nearby, she looked up to see one of the green dragons locked in a battle with a deep red one. "After thy call, I felt further assistance than my own would be required," said a familiar voice from behind her. She turned, immensely grateful to see Maldor had arrived. "Aieden, whom thou see here, and

Teslyn, an ice dragon, answered. I would suggest thou seek safety, young one, as the battle is likely to grow violent."

"I can't find my father, or my friend Cai," she said. "I'm not running and hiding while they're still out here."

Maldor inclined his head. "Then put thine arts to good use, Enkarini." He took off, flying straight at another of the green dragons and forcing it away from the square.

Enkarini stared upwards, uncertain of what exactly she could do for anyone here. She heard shouts from the street ahead and saw a house in flames with people trapped inside. She ran over, calling up one of the few water spells she knew, and helped douse the fire at least enough for the family inside to get out.

Two huge, roaring shadows flew overhead, and everyone scattered. Enkarini ran as green fire scorched the street, and the ground shook violently beneath her. She dived through a door that had been left open, crawled under a table and focused on home. Perhaps Caiara and Harndak had made it back there. The sitting room popped into her mind, empty as they had left it when they went to join the party. She moved her attention to her father, and saw him in the street outside the forge, yelling her name. Caiara stood near him, an almost constant stream of ice flying from her hands as she battled the flames around them. *Cai! I'm in the market square!* she thought frantically to her friend.

"She's in the market square!" Caiara shouted to Harndak. He nodded and ran in that direction, leaping over a wooden beam as Enkarini let her vision fade.

She scrabbled out from under the table and back out into the street. At least the ground had stopped shaking here, and she picked her way through the debris and chaos back to the square. The ferocious roars of battling dragons and the desperate shrieks of frightened people echoed all around, laid over a background of crashing stones and rushing fire, but the square itself was deserted. Enkarini stood on the remains of a stall, looking for her father, listening for any sound that might indicate approaching danger.

The sound of flapping wings reached her, but in the cacophony, it took her a moment to pinpoint its source. She leapt off the charred stall, ready to defend herself, but realised a second too late that it had come from behind her.

"Move!" someone shouted, and she had barely turned when a body slammed into her, knocking her aside. She caught a glimpse of her father, soot-streaked and panicked, before the dragon's emerald flames engulfed him. It was over in a matter of seconds, the burnt form crumbling to the ground.

Time seemed to freeze, and an icy rage took hold of the girl. Thick black smoke gathered around her, and without thinking she pulled it into herself. A fierce, hot wind blew out of nowhere and wrapped around her, whipping her hair around her face and tugging at her clothes. She rose into the air gracefully, her arms outstretched and darkness swirling around her, until she was level with the dragon that had killed her father. She screamed, and the shadows flew from her hands to swarm over the green dragon in front of her. It struggled, tearing at the smoke with its claws and teeth, but within a few moments it was subdued and resting on the ground.

Enkarini was lost in the magic that had gripped her, almost using her as a vessel, and sought out another of the dragons attacking the town. Maldor had joined her, and together they brought two more green dragons under control before the girl fell back to the ground. Aieden and Teslyn were still battling two of the remaining green dragons overhead, and they seemed to be trying to draw them away from Tewen. Enkarini had lost interest in the battle though and stumbled through the streets back to the place her father had fallen.

Harndak lay in the centre of a ring of destruction, as though something had simply blown the debris of the battle away from him. She fell to her knees beside him, distantly aware of the cries around her and the wetness on her own face. This wasn't real, it couldn't be, her father was only joking around and he would sit up in a minute, smile at her and hug her. Why was he just lying there? Why didn't he get up already, because he wasn't dead, he wasn't... "Daddy, please get up," she whimpered. It felt like an eternity, staring at the blackened form that had been her father, and she wept as though her tears would revive him.

The great dark shape of Maldor landed beside her, and she turned to him desperately. She rubbed her sleeve over her eyes and nose, smearing the tears rather than drying them. "We can bring him back, right? You said that it had been done, that other dragon had broken the veil, raised the dead and..."

Maldor shook his head. "I am deeply sorry, young one. If there were a way to return thy father to life, I would do so in an instant. However, while powerful magic may raise the body and give it a semblance of life, there is no spell to restore the soul, the essence of the person, not in the way thou would wish it."

Enkarini turned away, fresh tears spilling from her eyes. Someone knelt beside her and pulled her close; she recognised Kandrina's perfume and returned the fierce hug. "It's not fair, it's not fair!" she cried, pressing her face into her sister's shoulder.

Kandrina said nothing, for what could be said? Enkarini was right, it wasn't fair, but nothing in life ever was. People all around them wailed in despair, pain and loss; many lives had been lost in the attack, the two sisters were by no means the only ones grieving, but this was the first death Enkarini was truly aware of. She had been only a few months old when their mother had gone, and although she had been old enough to understand that her brother was dead a few years ago, she had not really grasped the full, ugly truth of that. Hearing that someone would never come home again was completely different from seeing them perish in front of you. As the girl's tears soaked her shirt, Kandrina gazed for the last time at her father. Slowly, she gathered her little sister into her arms as she had when Enkarini was small and carried her away. It would do neither of them any good to remain by the burned, broken body any longer.

She walked without any real destination in mind except *away*, away from the hysterical cries of grief and the stench of flames and blood, away from the stilled forms of their father and so many others. Enkarini's weight kept her aware of her surroundings, and although she was really too heavy to be carrying for long, Kandrina was glad of the strain in her arms and the dampness on her shoulder. As she left the centre of town, she saw people with carts already starting to gather the fallen. There were too many to hold individual funerals, most of them would be buried in a mass grave within a day. She refused to think of whether Harndak would be among them.

Eventually she reached a quiet street on the outskirts of Tewen; the green dragons had not reached this part of town, and the air was clear. She sank onto a low wall around someone's garden, and finally put her sister down. Her own eyes were oddly dry; the tears would come later, in private. Now, she knew, she had to be strong and steady for Enkarini. She wilfully ignored for a moment the frightening surge of magic that had come from the girl, blasting everything in her vicinity; she had a feeling Enkarini did not understand it herself, but she knew her sister would never have intentionally caused harm to anyone or anything.

A door opened nearby. "Is it over?" someone called nervously. "Have those beasts left us alone?"

Kandrina turned to look at the man climbing out of the dome in the garden behind her. She merely nodded to him; he could work out what had happened for himself. Right now, her only concern was for her sister. "Enkarini?" she whispered softly.

The girl slowly released Kandrina's shirt and looked at her. "It's really real, isn't it," she said in a very small voice. Kandrina could only nod. "Father's gone because of me. He pushed me out of the way and got hit himself," she wailed.

"Listen to me," Kandrina said firmly. "This is not your fault. Don't you dare blame yourself. Father chose to save you because he loved you, and that's what parents do. They always put their children first, even if it means they're hurt instead. None of this is your fault." She pulled Enkarini into another hug, needing the comfort just as much herself.

She sniffled against Kandrina's shoulder. "I don't know what happened to me. I didn't mean to do any of that, I didn't want to hurt anyone," she cried.

Kandrina held her tightly. "Shh. I

know. You didn't hurt anyone, you were helping against those green dragons," she whispered softly as she stroked the girl's hair. A few moments passed, and gradually Enkarini's sobs faded away. She stepped back a little, and seemed about to say something, when a group of people charged around the corner towards them.

"There she is! The black witch, I saw her aiding those beasts with her dark magic!" the woman at the front screamed. The mob, though small, was clearly fuelled by hysterical fear.

Kandrina stood in front of her sister, shielding her as best as she could. "She was fighting the dragons, that was clear for anyone to see!" she yelled back. "Go back and take a look, her supposedly dark magic is still binding them and keeping them under control!" She prepared herself to reach for her sword; though she didn't want to attack these people, who were really just frightened of something they didn't understand, she would always protect her sister.

"Mother, that's enough!" someone else shouted from behind her. Kandrina turned to see a girl with short, reddish-blonde hair glaring at the woman leading the mob. "Rini's done nothing wrong, you're the one trying to hurt people here." She marched up to stand beside Kandrina.

The woman blanched. "Caiara, get away from them. The black witch has a Demon spawn protecting her," she said harshly.

Kandrina almost rolled her eyes. *Demon spawn?* She thought those insults had finished when people learnt about the Colourless. "My sister is not a black witch," she snapped.

"Hey, bitch," another voice shouted. "If you want to see what real black magic is like, I can show you." It was a tall, black-haired boy, his eyes fixed on the mob and a sneer twisting his pointed, rodentine face. He almost seemed to hover across the street to join Kandrina and Caiara in front of Enkarini, his hands lined with flames as he stared the woman down.

The girl called Caiara turned to him, her hands on her hips. "For pity's sake, Soris, you really think that's going to help?" She shook her head at him and looked back at the mob. "She's my friend, and I know she's a good person. You're just afraid of something that doesn't fit into your own view," she shouted at her mother.

"They've twisted your mind, Caiara, led you away from the path you needed to follow," the woman called out. "I should have known you would be trouble when you started having those wicked visions; clearly even the temple couldn't save you."

"That will do, Aila. Your daughter did not need saving to begin with, I have tried to explain this time and time again," said another woman, emerging from a side street to stand beside the four of them. She had long brown hair piled on top of her head and wore the robes of a high priestess. "Caiara has a wonderful gift, as do all of the students at our Library. Some may need more specialised training than others, but I assure you that none of them are wicked or dangerous. If you would be so kind as to cease attacking my pupils and disband your lynch mob, I will gladly discuss this with you at a later date. We have all been through enough today, I believe."

Most of the small gang had filtered away by this point, leaving Aila with only half a dozen rather scolded-looking followers. She chewed her bottom lip, her eyes flicking between the priestess and Caiara, before turning and leaving without another word. Kandrina relaxed her grip on her sword, immeasurably glad that she had not needed it.

The priestess knelt, looking at Enkarini. "You did a very good thing today; don't let anyone tell you otherwise. If you need to talk, I'll be here to listen," she said. "You will always be welcome at the Library, and I do hope you will return to share what you learn on the other side."

Enkarini stared at her. "You know that we opened the gate?"

"Of course. Little happens in my temple without my knowledge, and I have been keeping a particularly close eye on you three of late." The priestess stood, her expression one of pride and admiration. "For now though, I have much to do; this attack has left many in need. I am glad I brought the students when I was called to help, this devastation will need many hands to repair it." She bade them all farewell and left.

Kandrina turned to the two who had

arrived to stand with her. "You're my sister's friends?" she asked.

The girl nodded. "We all study at the Library together. What happened?"

"Our father..." Kandrina couldn't finish the sentence. "Enkarini saw it happen." Both of them dropped their gazes.

Enkarini slowly turned to face her friends. "Cai, thanks for standing up for me just now. And you, Soris. But your mother was right, Cai, I was doing black magic. I wasn't even in control of it," she whispered.

"So what?" Soris asked. "Why does it matter if it was black magic? You still stopped three of those dragons basically on your own, that's pretty good if you ask me. You can learn to control it. You already used it to protect people, not to hurt people. That can't be a bad thing."

Caiara nodded. "This is the only time you'll hear me admit it, but he's right. You can't let some stupid superstition get to you, Rini."

Kandrina swept her sister into another tight hug. "Listen to your friends. Now, let's get off these streets before someone else forms a mob." She started walking down the road toward Remlik's place, then stopped and turned to the other two. "You two as well. I know Caiara was staying at Father's, and any friend of my sister's is welcome at our house." They both smiled faintly and followed her.

Epilogue

The sisters knelt by the headstone, shining and new, next to their mother's and brother's. The grave was empty, their father buried in the mass grave on the plains alongside the dozens of other victims of the dragon attack. They had erected the stone as a memorial rather than a marker; a place where their father's name would stand forever alongside those of his wife and son.

"I'm leaving." Enkarini spoke softly, as though afraid of disturbing anyone. "Once the forge is sold, and everything's settled. Maldor offered to teach me how to use my magic, and there's not much left for me here."

Kandrina raised an eyebrow. "Thanks," she mumbled, without any real hurt. She could see why her sister wanted to get away; she herself was going with Remlik and his sister to the new university in Yoscar next week.

They looked at each other. "I didn't mean it like that," Enkarini said. "I just... I need to learn how to control this, and there's nobody here who can teach me. It won't be forever, just until I can use this properly. What happened after... when Father... I wasn't in control of it, it just exploded around me."

"I understand; you don't have to explain." Kandrina reached out and put her arm around the younger girl. "Keep in touch though; someone's got to worry about you, on your own out there, living with a bunch of dragons."

Enkarini gave a quiet chuckle. "Who'd have thought you'd turn out to be the sensible one?"

"I'm as surprised as anyone," Kandrina stood slowly and brushed some loose grass from her knees. Enkarini did the same, and for a few moments the two sisters watched each other in silence. It suddenly struck Kandrina that she was no longer looking down at her little sister; Enkarini had grown rapidly over the last year, and if anything was now slightly taller than her. "Take care of yourself up there, and tell those dragons if anything happens to you, they'll have to answer to me," Kandrina said with a faint smile.

"I will do," Enkarini replied. "I think some of the others from the Library are coming as well, and I know Cai wants to go, so I'll have at least one friend with me, and High Priestess Glissia wants Arikele to go and start working some things out with the mages up there. You look after Remlik and Remlika, don't let them get too wrapped up in studying."

They looked down at the gravestone, a silent goodbye passing between them. Enkarini conjured a wreath and laid it on the ground before walking away. There was nothing more she wanted to say, nothing she could say; the grief was too fresh, things she had once thought important seemed trivial in the wake of their loss. She felt tears running down her cheeks again and wiped them away. The words her sister had said after Perlak's funeral finally made sense to her; there was no point in crying over the dead, it would not bring them back, it would not change anything that had happened. The only thing she could do was find a way to prevent it happening again.

Kandrina watched her sister leave, a

twist of regret in her heart at the thought that they had not spent enough time together. She had been too busy with her own life, her adventures and her studies, to spend any real time with her family over the last few years. Now the only remaining family she had was going to the other side of the world. Hot tears stung the corners of her eyes, as she finally had the privacy to weep. She cried for more than her father; both sisters' lives had been altered during the battle, and there was no way to turn back and recapture their lost selves, to undo the events that had broken the last of their childhoods. Things would never be the same again.